*A Table of Green Fields*

*Also by Guy Davenport*

FICTION
Tatlin!
Da Vinci's Bicycle
Eclogues
Trois Caprices
Apples and Pears
The Bicycle Rider
The Jules Verne Steam Balloon
The Drummer of the Eleventh North Devonshire Fusiliers

ESSAYS
The Geography of the Imagination
Every Force Evolves a Form
A Balthus Notebook

POETRY
Flowers and Leaves
Thasos and Ohio

TRANSLATIONS
Archilochos Sappho Alkman: Three Greek Poets
The Mimes of Herondas
Anakreon
Herakleitos and Diogenes

# GUY DAVENPORT

*A Table of Green Fields*

TEN STORIES

A NEW DIRECTIONS BOOK

ACKNOWLEDGMENTS

"August Blue" was first published in *Antaeus* and later as a book by the Larkspur Press (Frankfort, Kentucky). "Belinda's World Tour" was first published in *The Santa Monica Review* and later as a book in a limited edition by Barry Magid at his Dim Gray Bar Press, with drawings by Deborah Norden. The Chinese ode in "The Concord Sonata" was first published in Gregory and Birgit Stephenson's magazine *Pearl* (Copenhagen). "O Gadjo Niglo" appeared in an earlier version in *Conjunctions*. To these editors and publishers I am grateful for their kind permission to reprint.

Manufactured in the United States of America
New Directions Books are printed on acid-free paper
First published clothbound by New Directions in 1993
Published simultaneously in Canada by Penguin Books Canada Limited

**Library of Congress Cataloging-in-Publication Data**
Davenport, Guy.
    A table of green fields : ten stories / by Guy Davenport.
      p.   cm.
    ISBN 0–8112–1251–3
    I. Title.
    PS3554.A86T28   1993
    813'.54—dc20                    93–18677
                                      CIP

New Directions Books are published for James Laughlin
by New Directions Publishing Corporation,
80 Eighth Avenue, New York 10011

# Contents

*A Table of Green Fields*

# August Blue

On the way to school, just past the bird market, there is one of
the largest fig trees in Jerusalem. It was believed by some to be
as old as the temple and to have a special blessing on it whereby
its figs were fatter and sweeter than any others in the world,
except, of course, those in the Garden of Eden. They were, in
color, more blue than green. The milk that bled from its stems
when you pulled one of its figs cured warts, the quinsy, and
whooping cough.

Schoolboys could see this great fig tree. A red wall, however, kept them from helping themselves to the occasional fig,
even though Roman law said that a traveler, or a child, could
pick an apple, pear, or fig, for refreshment, without being
guilty of theft, and the Torah was equally lenient and understanding of the hunger of travelers and boys.

On a fine morning in the month of Tishri, Daniel, Yaakov,
and Yeshua, having inspected finches and quail in cages, and
leapfrogged in the narrowest streets, shouted at by merchants,
gave their usual longing looks at the fig tree.

—If only figs, Daniel said, knocked down like apples, and if we
had a pole.

—But they don't, Yaakov said. And they wouldn't fall in the
street, anyway.

They sighed, all three.

—Figs and dates smushed together with ewe milk, and roasted
barley sprinkled on top, Yeshua said.

—Figs and honey, Daniel said.

—Figs just so, juicy and ripe, said Yaakov.

—What do you *say* to the donkeys? Daniel asked.

It was a game of Yeshua's to stop along the way to school and whisper into donkeys' ears, something quick and confidential, with a knowing smile. The donkeys never failed to quicken, lift their ears, and stare at him.

—Behold the grandfather of all jackrabbits! he would say out loud.

—I tell them something they think I don't know, Yeshua said. I spoke to the quail, too.

—Yeshua's *meshuggeh*.

—Want a fig? Yeshua said. One for each of you. Close your eyes and hold out your hands.

—You've got figs for recess?

—No, I got them off the tree back there.

Daniel looked at Yaakov, Yaakov at Daniel.

—So don't believe me, Yeshua said.

With a flourish of his hand he showed them a plump blue fig in his fingers. He gave it to Daniel. Another twirl and wiggle of fingers, and there was a fig for Yaakov.

—Holy Moses!

—Don't swear, Yeshua said. There's Zakkaiah looking up and down the street for us.

They ran to the school gate, herded in by their teacher, Zakkaiah, whose beard was combed and who smelled of licorice. They sat on cushions on a clean wooden floor, in a semicircle before Zakkaiah, who sat on a stool.

—*Alef*, Zakkaiah said.

—It's an ox, said Daniel.

—It comes first, a boy named Nathan said.

—So listen, said Zakkaiah.

He explained the derivation of *alef* from the old Phoenician alphabet, and talked about the versatility of a set of signs that could graph speech, contrasting it to the barbarous syllabaries of the Egyptians and the Assyrians.

—Greek is an even further advance. Their *alpha*, however, is not our *alef*. They have letters for their vowels, and use their *alpha* for one of them. Micah, what letter comes next?

—*Beth*.

—Yeshua! Zakkaiah said, are you chewing something?

—A fig.

—And what kind of manners is it to eat figs when we are learning the alphabet?

Nathan, who had just been slipped a fig by Yeshua, tucked it inside his blouse and looked innocent. Amos, who was also eating a fig passed back to him by Yeshua, swallowed his whole.

—And what is *beth*, Micah?

—But Teacher, Yeshua said, we have not learned what is to be known about *alef*, and here we are hastening on to *beth*.

Zakkaiah's mouth fell open.

—So? he said. You want me to forget that you were having a late breakfast rather than paying attention to the lesson?

—Oh no, Teacher.

—I'm listening to what you have to say about *alef*, if you're quite through eating figs.

Yeshua worked his fingers in the air until there was a fig in them.

—Have a fig for yourself, O Teacher. And another. And yet another. They are from the great tree down the street, and are the juiciest and tastiest figs in all Jerusalem.

Zakkaiah stood with the three figs in his cupped hands, staring at Yeshua, speechless. He looked at the figs and he looked at Yeshua.

—My father sent them to you, O Teacher. They are good for the bowels, he says.

A silence.

—I will thank him when I see him, Zakkaiah said in a soft voice.

—*Alef*, Yeshua said. I will recite about *alef*.

There was an uneasiness in the class. Zakkaiah was obviously thinking several things at once.

—*Alef!* Yeshua said in a voice pitched bright. In the *alef* there's a *yud* up here, and a *yud* down there, with a line between. As with all boundaries, this line both joins and separates. The *yud* above is the Creator of the universe, of the earth, the sun, the moon, the planets, and the stars. The *yud* below is us, the people. The line between is the Torah, the prophets, the law. It is the eye for seeing what we can of the Creator. He is evident in his work, the world.

—You are reciting a commentary, Zakkaiah said, but whose?

—I'm making it up, Yeshua said. The Creator made us creators, too. Look at the spider knitting its web and at the bird building its nest. Every work has a maker.

—Is it the blessed Hillel your father has taught you?

—Who is Hillel? The alphabet is all pictures. You can look at them and see what they are: a house, a camel. The *alef* is a picture of the whole world. Cool water on dusty feet, that's a grand thing, and the smell of wood shavings and a crust dunked in wine, and honey, and dancing to the tabor and flute. These good things belong down here, but they come from up there. That's why there's a line between the top *yud* and the bottom *yud*. Everything has a fence, so we can know where it is. A house has rooms, a garden has a wall.

Zakkaiah sat on his stool, hard. He stuck the fingers of his left hand into his beard. His right hand held three figs.

—But the fun of the line between the *yuds*, Yeshua went on, is that it's a fence only if you look at it that way. It is really a road, and like all roads it goes both ways. You have to know which way you're going. Look at the anemones that make the fields red all of a sudden after the first rain of the wet season. The grand dresses at Solomon's court were not such a sight, and they were made with looms and needles, whereas the master of the universe made the anemones overnight, with a word. You can get near the line with much labor, or you can cross it with a step.

—I told you Yeshua's *meshuggeh*, Daniel whispered to Yaakov.

—Why don't you eat your figs, O Teacher? Yeshua asked. I have more.

2

On a blustery late afternoon in March 1842, Professor James Joseph Sylvester of the University of Virginia was walking along a brick path across the lawn in front of Jefferson's Rotunda. He had been brought from London to teach mathematics only the November before, and still wondered at these neoclassical buildings set in an American forest, and at the utilitarian rowhouse dormitories, at the black slaves who dressed the students and carried their books to class. He taught arithmetic and algebra from Lacroix's serviceable manual, trigonometry, geometry, the calculus differential and integral. Next term he was offering a course from Poisson's *Mechanics* and Laplace's *Mécanique céleste*.

He was a member of the Royal Society. At age twenty-seven he had distinguished himself with so brilliant a series of mathematical papers that he had been invited to come to Virginia. Jefferson's plan was to bring the best minds of Europe to dwell in his academic village, as he liked to call it. And now Jefferson was dead, leaving his faculty of European geologists, chemists, linguists, historians, and mathematicians to carry on his work of civilizing Virginia and her sister states.

Professor Sylvester's problem was one he had never before met. His students, all healthy, strapping young men from the richest of families, were illiterate. They knew nothing. He could scarcely understand a word they said. They came late to class, if at all, accompanied by their slaves. They talked with each other while Professor Sylvester lectured. The strangest thing about them was that they did not want to learn. Take Ballard. He was from Louisiana, some great plantation with hundreds of slaves. He was a handsome lad, beautifully dressed. Yet if called upon, he would say:

—I could answer that, Fesser, if I wanted to, but frankly I'm not minded to do so.

—Is this not insolence, Mr. Ballard?

—If you were a gentleman, Fesser, you'd know how to talk to one, now wouldn't you?

A roar of laughter.

He had gone to the faculty. They told him that the students had reduced Jefferson to tears, that they had shot three professors already, that he had best deal with them as patiently as he knew how. There was no support to be expected from Charlottesville, which was of the opinion that the faculty was composed of atheists, Catholics, Jews, Jesuits. A Hungarian professor had had to leave town in the dark of night.

They dueled, and fought with Bowie knives. They drank themselves into insensibility. They came to class drunk. When Sylvester tried to find out why this was allowed, he was reminded that the students were aristocrats.

—Mr. Ballard, will you rehearse Euclid's proofs for the Pythagorean theorem of the right triangle?

—Suck my dick.

He had had to ask what the words meant, and blushed. On the advice of a fellow professor he had bought a sword cane. One never knew. He was paid handsomely, but what worried him was that the papers he had been writing were harder and harder to finish. He was famous for averaging a mathematical paper a month. He knew that he had the reputation among his peers of having the most fertile genius of his generation. He was a Mozart of mathematics. He was finding it embarrassing to keep up his correspondence with the few men in Germany, France, and England who understood his work. These barbarian louts with their slaves and dueling pistols were making him sterile, and that tore at his soul more than their childish disrespect and leaden ignorance.

Why were they here, at a university, at least a university in name and intent? The French professor was slowly losing his mind, as none of his students had learned two words together of French. They gambled all night, knifed each other at dawn, drank until they puked.

And on this March afternoon Professor Sylvester found

himself approaching the brothers Weeks, Bill and Al, or Mr. William and Mr. Alfred Weeks, gentlemen, as he must address them in class. They wore yellow and green frock coats, with flowery weskits. They were smoking long black cigars, and carried their top hats in their hands.

—You ain't a-going to speak to us, Jewboy?

Thus William, the elder of the brothers.

—Sir! said Sylvester.

—Yes, Fesser Jew Cockney, said Alfred. If you're going to teach rithmatic and that damn calc'lus shit to gentlemen, you ought to take off your hat to them when you meet us on the lawn, oughtn't he, Bill?

—Sir! said Sylvester.

—May be, said William Weeks, that if we pulled the fesser's Jew hat down over his Jew chin, he'd remember next time to speak to gentlemen.

Sylvester drew his sword from his cane with one graceful movement, and with another drove it into Alfred Weeks's chest.

Alfred screamed.

William ran.

Alfred fell backward, groaning:

—O Jesus! I have met my fatal doom!

Professor Sylvester coolly sheathed his sword, tapped it on the brick walk to assure that it was firmly fitted in his cane, turned on his heel, and walked away. He went to his rooms, packed a single suitcase, and walked to the posthouse to wait for a stage to Washington. This he boarded, when it came.

Alfred Weeks writhed on the brick walk, crying like a baby, calling for instant revenge. William came back with a doctor, who was mystified.

—Have you been bit by a m'skeeter, son? They ain't no wound. There's a little tear in your weskit, as I can see, and a kind of scratch here on your chest, like a pinprick.

—You mean I ain't killed dead?

Sylvester retrenched in New York City, where he practiced law. The mathematical papers began to be written again. He was called to the Johns Hopkins University, where he founded the first school of mathematics in the United States, where he arranged for the first woman to enter an American graduate school, where he argued with Charles Sanders Peirce, and where he introduced the Hebrew letters *shin* and *teth* into mathematical annotation.

Years later, the great Georg Cantor, remembering Sylvester, introduced the letter *alef* as a symbol of the transfinite.

3

As we descended westward, we saw the fen country on our right, almost all covered with water like a sea, the Michaelmas rains having been very great that year, they had sent down great floods of water from the upland countries, and those fens being, as may be very properly said, the sink of no less than thirteen counties; that is to say, that all the water, or most part of the water of thirteen counties falls into them.

The people of that place, which if they be born there they call the Breedlings, sometimes row from one spot to another, and sometimes wade.

In these fens are abundance of those admirable pieces of art called duckoys; that is to say, places so adapted for the harbor and shelter of wild fowl, and then furnished with decoy ducks, who are taught to allure and entice their kind to the places they belong to. It is incredible what quantities of wild fowl of all sorts they take in these duckoys every week during the season, duck, mallard, teal, and widgeon.

As these fens are covered with water, so I observed too that they generally at this latter part of the year appear also covered with fogs, so that when the downs and higher grounds of the adjacent country were gilded by the beams of the sun, the Isle of Ely looked as if wrapped up in blankets, and nothing to be seen, but now and then, the lanthorn or cupola of Ely Minster.

## 4

Now the bike that was idling down the sheepwalk to the cove as sweet as the hum of a bee was a Brough, we saw, Willy and I. The rider of it lifted his goggles, which had stenciled a mask of clean flesh on the dust and ruddle of his face. A long face with shy blue eyes it was, and his light hair was blown back. He wore a Royal Air Force uniform and was, like we judged, a private.

Willy asked if he was lost or had come on purpose, after naming the bike a Brough and the uniform RAF, showing that he knew both by sight.

—Right and right, the motorcyclist said.

He spoke Oxford.

—I'm here on purpose if I've found Tuke the painter's, though I shan't disturb him if he's busy. I wrote him last week.

—Aye, the penny postal, I remembered. He was interested in it.

—Name's Ross, the cyclist said.

—Sainsbury here, Willy said. My mate's Georgie Fouracre.

We all nodded, fashionable-like.

—Mr. Tuke, I said, is down yonder, in the cove, with Leo Marshall, painting of him in and out of a dory. If your postal named today, he'll be expecting you. We get the odd visitor from London, time to time, and some from up north and the continent.

So we rolled the motorbike down to Mr. Tuke and Leo. The canvas was on the easel, the dory on the strand, and Leo was drawing off worsted stockings, brown as a nut all over.

For all of his having the lines of a Dane, this airman Ross was uncommonly short. The crinkle of Mr. Tuke's eyes showed how pleased he was. His blue beret and moustache, his French blouse and sailor's breeks made one kind of contrast with the tight drab uniform Ross seemed to be bound in, with no give at all anywhere, and horse-blanket tough, and Leo's want of a stitch made another.

Ross was interested in the picture on the easel, which was

the one that got named *Morning Splendour*, two of us in a dory and me on the strand as naked as the day I came into the world. It hangs in Baden-Powell House, in London, bought by the Boy Scouts. The color harmonies are the same as those of the more famous *August Blue* that's in the Tate.

This visit of Ross's was a summer morning in 1922. And a nice little watercolor came of it, of Ross undressing for a swim. Except that it isn't Ross.

What was it about him? He was at ease with us, as many are not, but he wasn't at ease with himself. Tuke got on with his painting. He posed Leo with a leg up on the dory.

—And your hand on your knee, just so. Turn a bit so that the light runs gold down your chest and left thigh.

He explained to Ross how he made quick watercolor studies, light being fugitive.

—There's nothing here, you know, but color. Light on a boy's back can be as mercurial as light on the sea.

Ross, it turned out as they talked, knew a lot about painters. He said that Augustus John is a crack draftsman but that of light and air he knows nothing.

Tuke smiled, and then he laughed, with his head back.

—These modernists. Ah, yes.

—And Wyndham Lewis paints a world that has neither air nor light.

—Do you know Lewis?

—I've met him. I dropped over his garden wall one evening. He was drawing in a back room. I introduced myself. It gave him quite a start. A childish trick on my part, but it amused him immensely. He fancies eccentricity.

He mentioned Eric Kennington, Rothenstein, Lamb. At one point Tuke gave him a very hard stare.

When Willy and I undressed, horsing around, as was our way, Ross paced as he talked with Tuke, holding his left wrist and wrenching it, as if he were screwing it off and on. He talked about Mantegna's bathing soldiers, which we had a print of in the studio, and a bathing place called Parson's Pleasure at Ox-

ford. He was like a professor with a subject. One thing re-
minded him of another, and he thought out loud about it.
—Oh yes, well, Eakins in America. No one can get near him,
Tuke said.
—Things return, Ross said. Here in the autumn of time you are
recovering a spring which we have forgotten in our culture, a
spring we know about in Greece and in the late Middle Ages.
   Did Tuke know a man named Huizinga? A Dutchman.
—Meredith, Tuke said, has a lovely scene of boys bathing, in
*Feverel*.
   It was Leo, stretching between poses, who asked Ross
why, if he was as educated as he sounded, he wasn't an officer.
—Cowardice, probably, Ross said.
—Leo didn't mean that in an untoward way, did you, Leo?
—Lord, no.
   The sea had taken on a wonderful green brightness, a
shuffling of silver, and the sky was glorious in its blue. Willy
had swum out, dog-paddling. Tuke had removed his scarf. I
was beginning to ponder what this visit of the little soldier
Ross was all about. Tuke seemed to know things about him
that we didn't, and to be keeping a secret. A confidence, perhaps
I should say.
   Willy did a devil dance on the sand, to get warm.
—We've often turned fair blue with cold for Mr. Tuke, he said.
   In many of the pictures where we all appear to be toasty
brown in fine sunlight we were actually freezing our bullocks
off.
—Will you pose, Aircraftsman Ross? Tuke said abruptly. I
covet your profile.
—I wonder, Ross said with a smile that was also a frown.
—We're a kind of *comitatus* here, Tuke said. Friends, all. The
vicar, who likes to visit at tea, usually when the boys are still
half undressed, has his doubts about the propriety of it all.
—Eats his doubts in muffins, Leo said, and drowns 'em in tea.
—He reads Housman, and Whitman.
—But brought back the Edward Carpenter we lent him without

a word to say about it.

I liked the mischief in Ross's eyes as he listened to all this.

—We are hypocritical dogs, we English.

—Decent, Leo said, patting his tranklements.

—A naked English lad is as decent as a calf, Willy said. Though the best painting I've posed for is fully clothed with Mary Baskins in the apple orchard.

—For which, Tuke said, I hope to be remembered, if at all, that and *August Blue.*

—It is insufferably egotistical, Ross said, unbuttoning his tunic, to assume that one cannot possibly be understood by another, or for that matter by people at large, but there is that residuum of privacy at our center which we do despair of exposing to the world's mercy.

Tuke thought that over carefully, very interested, you could tell by the cock of his head.

—True, he said. We aren't quite ready to admit that we are all alike, all human. And in our sameness we are wonderfully different.

His tunic open on an Aertex vest, Ross sat to unwind his leggings and to pull off his glossy hobnailed boots.

—I'm wondering, he said, what I've come here to find. I'm forever, I think, looking for one thing or another. When I first saw your painting, Tuke, I recognized a fellow spirit, and life is not so long that we can afford to put off meeting one's kin.

He shed his trousers, which had a complexity of buttons and flaps. Naked as Willy, Leo, and I, he seemed little more than a boy with a shock of hair and shy blue eyes. There was something wrong with his balls, as if they hadn't come down properly, or were stunted.

—Sit on the sand, Tuke said. I can do a crayon study fairly quickly.

—The sun feels good.

—Have you been drawn by any of these artists you've talked about?

—John. He did me in pencil. Kennington, pastel.

—Would it be a liberty, Leo said, as I had wanted to say, to pry into how a private in the RAF is so up on painters, sitting for them and all?

—There goes Leo again, Tuke said, drawing the thinnest possible line between good manners and intelligent curiosity.

—Oh, I don't mind, Ross grinned. The answer, Leo my fine fellow, is that I'm not Aircraftsman Ross 352087. The Brough is real, and the 352087 is real, and the uniform is real enough for the RAF. For the rest, I was born an impostor.

—Look straight ahead, and slightly up, Tuke said. I do hope the vicar doesn't turn up. He's well up on things, if you see what I mean.

—I don't, I said without thinking.

Tuke and Ross exchanged smiles.

—He would most probably recognize Private Ross.

—You're playing a teasing game with us, I said. Vicar, of all people! He didn't know Lord Gower when he was here with Frank or that French writer with the square face.

—Ross is different, Tuke said.

—Oh, I'm not afraid of the vicar, Ross said. I've got being an impostor down to an art. I've posed for a painter who didn't recognize me in the street the next day. The trick is to feel that you're nobody, and act accordingly.

—You've got to tell us, Leo said. You've gone too far not to.

—But, said Ross, there's really nothing to tell. I could tell you that my name is Chapman, which happens to be true, and you're none the wiser, are you? Things in this world are like that. A bloke whose name you know as Ross turns out to be named Chapman. It's worth Fanny Fuck All, as we say in barracks. Georgie Fouracre is Georgie Fouracre. You know who you are. You will beget strapping boys like yourself, and sit by your own fireside, you and your good wife.

—Mary Baskins, Leo said, more fool her.

—You lost your hopes with her by belching in church. Sounded like a bullfrog, and Vicar lost his place in Deuteronomy.

—But Vicar would recognize Chapman here, from the papers,

from the pictures, from knowing him?

—I've said quite enough, Tuke said. I've got the profile. What about a bathe, what say?

Tuke was out of his clothes in the shake of a lamb's tail. Ross swam well, effortlessly. It was Willy who said later that he did everything with style, as if there was the one right way of doing a thing.

We had no towels, and were sitting and drying in the sun when there were steps down the path, and here was Vicar, shouting jovially, using a wholly unnecessary brolly as a cane, fanning himself with a cream panama.

—Oh! I say.

—You've seen us mother-naked before, Vicar, Leo said, giving Willy's ribs an elbow.

—Oh, I say! Of course, of course. A painter of lads must have lads to paint. If I'm intruding, I shall beat a prudent retreat, what what?

—Not at all, Tuke said. As a matter of fact, I have been making a watercolor study of a visitor, who came on that motorbike, and whom I'd like you to meet.

—I noticed the motorbike, yes. The etiquette of meeting a gentleman in a state of nature is an interesting one which our nannies rather passed over lightly.

Ross rose with an easy dignity and shook Vicar's hand.

—The Reverend Button Milford, Tuke said. Aircraftsman Ross. He has sat for John and is kind enough to like my work.

—Ever so pleased, I'm sure, said Vicar. Don't get dressed on my account. A classical education gives one a taste for the, ah, pastoral, don't you know.

Vicar dithered about, causing Leo to search the horizon for, as may be, a ship. And then asked:

—Were you, Ross, in this late, and one hopes last, terrible war? But of course you weren't: you're too young.

—I was indeed in the war, Ross said. And it is not the last.

# Belinda's World Tour

A little girl, hustled into her pram by an officious nurse, discovered halfway home from the park that her doll Belinda had been left behind. The nurse had finished her gossip with the nurse who minced with one hand on her hip, and had had a good look at the grenadiers in creaking boots who strolled in the park to eye and give smiling nods to the nurses. She had posted a letter and sniffed at various people. Lizaveta had tried to talk to a little boy who spoke only a soft gibberish, had kissed and been kissed by a large dog, and had helped another little girl fill her shoes with sand.

And Belinda had been left behind. They went back and looked for her in all the places they had been. The nurse was in a state. Lizaveta howled. Her father and mother were at a loss to comfort her, as this was the first tragedy of her life and she was indulging all its possibilities. Her grief was the more terrible in that they had a guest to tea, Herr Doktor Kafka of the Assicurazioni Generali, Prague office.

—Dear Lizaveta! Herr Kafka said. You are so very unhappy that I am going to tell you something that was going to be a surprise. Belinda did not have time to tell you herself. While you were not looking, she met a little boy her own age, perhaps a doll, perhaps a little boy, I couldn't quite tell, who invited her to go with him around the world. But he was leaving immediately. There was no time to dally. She had to make up her mind then and there. Such things happen. Dolls, you know, are born in department stores, and have a more advanced knowledge than those of us who are brought to houses by storks. We have such a limited knowledge of things. Belinda did, in her haste, ask me to tell you that she would write, daily, and that she would have told you of her sudden plans if she had been able to find you in time.

Lizaveta stared.

But the very next day there was a postcard for her in the mail. She had never had a postcard before. On its picture side was London Bridge, and on the other lots of writing which her mother read to her, and her father, again, when he came home for dinner.

*

Dear Lizaveta: We came to London by balloon. Oh, how exciting it is to float over mountains, rivers, and cities with my friend Rudolf, who had packed a lunch of cherries and jam. The English are very strange. Their clothes cover all of them, even their heads, where the buttons go right up into their hats, with button holes, so to speak, to look out of, and a kind of sleeve for their very large noses. They all carry umbrellas, as it rains constantly, and long poles to poke their way through the fog. They live on muffins and tea. I have seen the King in a carriage drawn by forty horses, stepping with precision to a drum. More later. Your loving doll, Belinda.

*

Dear Lizaveta: We came to Scotland by train. It went through a tunnel all the way from London to Edinburgh, so dark that all the passengers were issued lanterns to read *The Times* by. The Scots all wear kilts, and dance to the bagpipe, and eat porridge which they cook in kettles the size of our bathtub. Rudolf and I have had a picnic in a meadow full of sheep. There are bandits everywhere. Most of the people in Edinburgh are lawyers, and their families live in apartments around the courtrooms. More later. Your loving friend, Belinda.

*

Dear Lizaveta: From Scotland we have traveled by steam packet to the Faeroe Islands, in the North Sea. The people here are all fisherfolk and belong to a religion called The Plymouth Brothers, so that when they aren't out in boats hauling in nets full of herring, they are in church singing hymns. The whole island rings with music. Not a single tree grows here, and the houses have rocks on their roofs, to keep the wind from blowing them away. When we said we were from Prague, they had never heard of it, and asked if it were on the moon. Can you imagine! This card will be slow getting there, as the mail boat comes but once a month. Your loving companion, Belinda.

\*

Dear Lizaveta: Here we are in Copenhagen, staying with a nice gentleman named Hans Christian Andersen. He lives next door to another nice gentleman named Søren Kierkegaard. They take Rudolf and me to a park that's wholly for children and dolls, called Tivoli. You can see what it looks like by turning over this card. Every afternoon at 4 little boys dressed in red (and they are all blond and have big blue eyes) march through Tivoli, and around and around it, beating drums and playing fifes. The harbor is the home of several mermaids. They are very shy and you have to be very patient and stand still a long time to see them. The Danes are melancholy and drink lots of coffee and read only serious books. I saw a book in a shop with the title *How To Be Sure As To What Is And What Isn't*. And *The Doll's Guide To Existentialism; If This, Then What?* and *You Are More Miserable Than You Think You Are* In haste, Belinda.

\*

Dear Lizaveta: The church bells here in St. Petersburg ring all day and all night long. Rudolf fears that our hearing will be affected. It snows all year round. There's a samovar in every streetcar. They read serious books here, too. Their favorite author is Count Tolstoy, who is one of his own peasants (they say this distresses his wife), and who eats only beets, though he adds an onion at Passover. We can't read a word of the shop signs. Some of the letters are backwards. The men have bushy beards and look like bears. The women keep their hands in muffs. Your shivering friend, Belinda.

*

Dear Lizaveta: We have crossed Siberia in a sled over the snow, and now we are on Sakhalin Island, staying with a very nice and gentle man whose name is Anton Chekhov. He lives in Moscow, but is here writing a book about this strange northern place where the mosquitoes are the size of parrots and all the people are in jail for disobeying their parents and taking things that didn't belong to them. The Russians are very strict. Mr. Chekhov pointed out to us a man who is serving a thousand years for not saying *Gesundheit* when the Czar sneezed in his hearing. It is all very sad. Mr. Chekhov is going to do something about it all, he says. He has a cat name of Pussinka who is anxious to return to Moscow and doesn't like Sakhalin Island at all, at all. Your loving friend, Belinda.

*

Dear Lizaveta: Japan! Oh, Japan! Rudolf and I have bought kimonos and roll about in a rickshaw, delighting in views of Fujiyama (a blue mountain with snow on top) through wisteria blossoms and cherry orchards and bridges that make a hump rather than lie flat. The Japanese drink tea in tiny cups. The women have tall hairdos in which they have stuck yellow sticks. Everybody stops what they are doing ten times a day to write a poem. These poems, which are very short, are about crickets and seeing Fujiyama through the wash on the line and about feeling lonely when the moon is full. We are very popular, as the Japanese like novelty. Excitedly, Belinda.

*

Dear Lizaveta: Here we are in China. That's the long wall on the other side of the card. The emperor is a little boy who wears a dress the color of paprika. He lives in a palace the size of Prague, with a thousand servants. To get from his nursery to his throne he has a chair between two poles, and is carried. Five doctors look at his poo-poo when he makes it. Sorry to be vulgar, but what's the point of travel if you don't learn how different people are outside Prague? Answer me that. The Chinese eat with two sticks and slurp their soup. Their hair is tied in pigtails. The whole country smells of ginger, and they say *plog* for Prague. All day long firecrackers, firecrackers, firecrackers! Your affectionate Belinda.

*

Dear Lizaveta: We have sailed to Tahiti in a clipper ship. This island is all pink and green, and the people are brown and lazy. The women are very beautiful, with long black hair and pretty black eyes. The children scamper up palm trees like monkeys and wear not a stitch of clothes. We have met a Frenchman name of Gauguin, who paints pictures of the Tahitians, and another Frenchman named Pierre Loti, who wears a fez and reads the European newspapers in the café all day and says that Tahiti is Romantic. What Rudolf and I say is that it's very hot and decidedly uncivilized. Have I said that Rudolf is of the royal family? He's a good sport, but he has his limits. There are no *streets* here! Romantically, Belinda.

*

Well! dear Lizaveta, San Francisco! Oh my! There are streets here, all uphill, and with gold prospectors and their donkeys on them. There are saloons with swinging doors, and Flora Dora girls dancing inside. Everybody plays *Oh Suzanna!* on their banjos (everybody has one) and everywhere you see Choctaws in blankets and cowboys with six-shooters and Chinese and Mexicans and Esquimaux and Mormons. All the houses are of wood, with fancy carved trimmings, and the gentry sit on their front porches and read political newspapers. Anybody in America can run for any public office whatever, so that the mayor of San Francisco is a Jewish tailor and his councilmen are a Red Indian, a Japanese gardener, a British earl, a Samoan cook, and a woman Presbyterian preacher. We have met a Scotsman name of Robert Louis Stevenson, who took us to see an Italian opera. Yours ever, Belinda.

*

Dear Lizaveta: I'm writing this in a stagecoach crossing the Wild West. We have seen many Indian villages of teepees, and thousands of buffalo. It took hours to get down one side of the Grand Canyon, across its floor (the river is shallow and we rolled right across, splashing) and up the other side. The Indians wear colorful blankets and have a feather stuck in their hair. Earlier today we saw the United States Cavalry riding along with the American flag. They were singing "Yankee Doodle Dandy" and were all very handsome. It will make me seasick to write more, as we're going as fast as a train. Dizzily, Belinda.

*

Dear Lizaveta: We have been to Chicago, which is on one of the Great Lakes, and crossed the Mississippi, which is so wide you can't see across it, only paddle-steamers in the middle, loaded with bales of cotton. We have seen utopias of Quakers and Shakers and Mennonites, who live just as they want to in this free country. There is no king, only a Congress which sits in Washington and couldn't care less what the people do. I have seen one of these Congressmen. He was fat (three chins, I assure you) and offered Rudolf and me a dollar each if we would vote for him. When we said we were from Prague, he said he hoped we'd start a war, as war is good for business. On to New York! In haste, your loving Belinda.

*

Dear Lizaveta: How things turn out! Rudolf and I are married! Oh yes, at Niagara Falls, where you stand in line, couple after couple, and get married by a Protestant minister, a rabbi, or a priest, take your choice. Then you get in a barrel (what fun!) and ride over the falls—you bounce and bounce at the bottom—

and rent a honeymoon cabin, of which there are hundreds around the falls, each with a happy husband and wife billing and cooing. I know from your parents that my sister in the department store has come to live with you and be your doll. Rudolf and I are going to the Argentine. You must come visit our ranch. I will remember you forever. Mrs. Rudolph Hapsburg und Porzelan (your Belinda).

# Gunnar and Nikolai

## 1

And, yes, the sailboat on a tack for Tisvilde under a tall blue sky piled high with summer clouds was, oh my, slotting through the Baltic at a speed which the calm day and rigged mainsail and jib could in no wise account for.

At the tiller, it was soon easy to see, sat a boy named Nikolai, fetching and trim. He took a beeline for the beach, into the rocky sand of which he crunched his prow, to the amazement of a hundred staring sunbathers.

Deftly lowering his sails with nonchalant ease, he folded them into smaller and smaller triangles, until they were no bigger than handkerchiefs. Then, with a snap here and a snap there, as if he were closing the sections of a folding ruler, whistling a melody by Luigi Boccherini as he worked, he collapsed the boat, mast, rigging, hull, keel, rudder and all, into a handful of sticks and cords. These he doubled over again and again, tucked them in with a napkin's worth of sails, and stuffed the lot into the zippered pocket of his windbreaker. His chart and compass he shoved into the pocket of his smitch of white pants. He rolled and squared his shoulders.

Indifferent to the astonished bathers, one of whom was having some species of fit, and to jumping and hooting children begging him to do it again, he strode with all the aplomb of his twelve years up the beach and across the road into the dark cool of the Troll Wood.

Søren Kierkegaard, most melancholy of Danes, used to walk here, a gnome among gnomes. An eagle in a spruce gazed at Nikolai with golden feral eyes, in acknowledgment of which he put both hands against a mountain pine, the tree friendly to spruce. Without one near, it would not grow. The eagle rolled a hunch into its shoulders, and Nikolai hugged the mountain pine.

A glance at the interplanetary mariner's chronometer on his left wrist alerted him to his appointment somewhere near Gray Brothers. So, with meadows and farms flickering past, he ran fifty kilometres in three seconds, slowing to a walk along Strøget.

A shoal of skateboarders flowed around him from the back as he passed a Peruvian gourd band, three games of chess that had been going on since the fourteenth century, and four fresh babies in a pram, each with a cone of ice cream.

The address was in an alley, once a very old street. The number was repeated on a wooden gate, which opened onto the place, one of the places, he'd been looking for all of his life.

Another was a cabin in Norway, deep in spruce and mountain pine near a steep fjord, where he could live like Robinson Crusoe, exactly as he pleased. A room of his very own, in Gray Brothers, free to come and go, to have friends in to spend the night and share hamburgers and polsers in the middle of the floor. A coffee plantation in Kenya. A lighthouse on a rock in the Orkneys, gulls blown past his windows, bleak dawns over a black sea, secure by a neat fire.

But this was just as good, a courtyard with a tree and rows and beds of flowers, a sculptor's studio with a pitched glass roof.

Along a pomp of dahlias in a line, rust mustard brick and yellow, he walked with a steady casualness to the blue door. A wicker basket beside it, for the mail. A stone jug with sweet williams. His mother was keen on botany, so he knew the names of flowers, weeds, and trees. And maybe an angel with nothing better to do would see him through this.

A card fixed to the door with a drawing pin: Gunnar Rung, the name Mama had said. He was about to push the doorbell when the door opened, wrecking his cool.

—Hello, he said in as deep a voice as he could manage, I'm Nikolai Bjerg.

The man who opened the door was tall, in jeans with a

true fit and an Icelandic sweater, and was much younger than Nikolai had expected. His eyes were as friendly as those of a large dog.

—You're on time, he said. Gunnar Rung here. Come in and let's see you.

Books, drawings on the walls, tables, an unfamiliar kind of furniture. And beyond, through wide double doors slid open, under a glass roof, a tall block of squared rock that must have been hauled in from an alley in back. Nikolai looked at as much as he could, all of it wonderfully strange and likable, with quick glances at Gunnar, who was goodlooking and had wads of rich brown curls, almost not Danish, and hands as big as a sailor's.

—It's an Ariel I have a commission for, Gunnar said walking around Nikolai, looking at him through framing hands. Your mother thought you might do, and would like posing. Have you ever posed before? It's not easy, and can be tedious and boring. There's also a King Matt I'm to do, a boy who's king of an unimaginable Poland, and you might also be him. We'll have to see how you and I get along. What about some coffee? Do you drink it?

—Sometimes. I mean, yes.

Coffee! Gunnar was treating him like a grown-up, so don't trash it.

—You can undress while I'm putting the coffee on. Won't take a minute.

—Everything? Nikolai asked, instantly regretting the question, unbuckling a scout's belt of green webbing, offering his charmingest and toothiest smile.

—That's the way the stone is to be, without a stitch.

Eyebrows bravely up, Nikolai backed out of his short denim pants and knelt to untie his gym shoes. Briefs and thick white socks he pulled off together. Then his jersey over his head.

—Two sugars? There's real cream. You'll get over blushing. Good knees, good toes.

—Sorry. Didn't think I'd blush. The statue will be the same
size as me? Hey! Good coffee, you know.
—Life size, oh yes. Keep turning around. Raise your free hand
and stretch. Do you think you can keep to a schedule for
posing?
—Sure. Why not? I really didn't think I'd go shy. Being
naked's fun. My grandma and grandpa, Mama's mama and
daddy, are Kropotkinites, and I'm boss in my own pants. My
folks are as broad-minded green as they come, no barbed wire
anywhere, good Danish liberals, to the point of being fussy.
You know what I mean?
      A mischievously knowing smile from Gunnar.
—Park your cup, there, and stand on your toes, arms over your
head. Legs out more, each side. We can't do a Thorvaldsen nor
yet an Eric Gill. I'm what they call a neoclassicist, a realist, and
out of it. What's being boss in your own pants mean?
—A licensed devil, according to Mama. Liberal points for what
boys do anyway, says Papa. Who's King Matt?
—Another character in a book, by a Polish doctor. Actually the
work will be of a boy carrying Matt's flag. At an awful moment.
I'll tell you all about it while we're working. You can read the
book.
      Eyes askew, Nikolai ran his tongue across the plump tilt
of his upper lip. While *we're* working.
—You have kids? I guess they're too little to pose.
      No, and no wife, either, just Samantha, whom you'll meet.
Arms out. Twist around to the right. You're going to do, you
know? You're Ariel, all right.


2


Nikolai sat on his clothes piled in a chair. Coffee break.
—Why was Ariel naked?
—He was a spirit of the air. Like an angel.
      Nikolai thought about this, guppying his coffee and
sprucing the fit of his foreskin.

—Angels wear lots of clothes. Bible clothes. Steen and Stoffer are neat today, did you see? I'll bet this Ariel you're copying me for had pure thoughts and never a hard on, right? There was a Steen and Stoffer where Steen sees monkeys in the zoo jacking off and he says *O gross!* and his mom and pop are suddenly interested in showing him the cockatoos and toucans. Parents.

—What a face, Gunnar said, running his fingers over his cast of Bourdelle's study of Herakles. The model was Doyen-Parigot, military bloke. Physical fitness enthusiast. Used to arrive on his horse at Bourdelle's in full soldierly fig.

—Looks like an opossum, wouldn't you say?

> *Punktum punktum,*
> *komma, streg!*
> *Sadan tegnes*
> *Nikolaj!*
>
> *Arme, ben,*
> *og mave stor.*
> *Sadan kom han*
> *til vor jord.*

—Killed at Verdun. You make Edith glance heavenward when you twitch your piddler. Christian Brother from the Faeroes she is, you know. Though I once had a girl model who played with herself as liberally as you, and as unconcerned for convention, and Edith rather took to leaning around the door to see, in passing.

—What's Verdun? You know Mikkel, the redhead kid, my pal, with terminal freckles and chipmunk teeth? His dad is all for his doing it every day. Says it keeps him happy.

—Verdun was a terrible battle in the First World War. Is Mikkel's daddy Ulf Tidselfnug? Break's over: back at it.

—Do you know him? He prints books. It's fun to go to Mikkel's, where, if we stay in his room, we can do anything we want to, and Mikkel's always answering the door in nothing

but a T-shirt and wrunkled socks. His mom says that if he
turns himself into an idiot how would you notice?
—O pure innocent Danish youtn!
     Questioning eyes.
—Teasing the model, Samantha said, is Gunnar's way of re-
lating. You'll get used to it. Besides, you can tease him back.
Gunnar's jealous, anyway.


TREE HOUSE

—How old is this Gunnar?
—He's had a rabbit, a Belgian hare I think it is, in a show, and
a naked girl holding one leg by the ankle in another. He did
those at the Academy, and then he was in Paris for a year. He
was seventeen when he went to the Academy, that's four years,
and Paris was just a couple of years back, so he's like twenty-
four, yuss? Outsized whacker in his jeans.
—The bint's there all the time?
—Oh no, very busy girl, Samantha. She comes and goes.
Spends the night a lot, too, I think.


     4

—Brancusi's *Torso of a Boy*, there. My Ariel is to be as pure
as that, but with all of you there, representational, as the critics
say, thugs, the lot of them.
     '     Nikolai tugged his foreskin into a snugger fit.
—It leks, and it doesn't, you know?
—The thighs make it a boy, and the hips the same girth as the
chest. But further than that, in style, you can't go. Gaudier,
here, had the genius of the age. Killed in the First World War,
only 24. That's his bust of the poet Pound, and that's his *Red
Dancer*.
—Real brainy is what I'm getting a reputation for, even at
home. Would Brancusi have used a model, some French soccer
player? He could at least have put in a navel. I'll have my
pecker and toms, won't I, as Ariel?

—Shakespeare would insist. He liked well-designed boys and approved of nature.

—I'll bet. Did Brancusi?

—Brancusi's private life is unknown. I think he simply worked, sawing and polishing and chiselling. He did his own cooking. There was a white dog named Polar.

—What would an Ariel by him have looked like?

5

Commandant Nikolai Doyen-Parigot rode his white charger Washington among Peugeots and Citroëns to Antoine Bourdelle's studio. Tying Washington to a parking meter, he strode inside. Bourdelle was in his smock. A boy was mixing modelling clay in a tub. Amidst life-size casts of Greek statues Nikolai Doyen-Parigot took off his uniform, handing it piece by piece, epauletted coat and sword and spurred boots and snowy white shirt and suspenders and wool socks slightly redolent of horse and long underwear, to a respectful but blushing concierge.

Herakles with the head of Apollo.

Thick curly hair matted his chest. His dick was as big as his charger's, and his balls were like two oranges in a cloth sack. His wife went around in a happy daze because of them, as did several lucky young actresses and dancers. Restocking the regiment for the next generation he called it.

He took the long bow that Bourdelle handed him and assumed the pose of Herakles killing the Stymphalian birds.

Later he would play soccer, and wrestle with Calixte Delmas. He would march his regiment up and down the street behind a military band.

—What are Stymphalian birds, Gunnar?

—Something Greek. Quit wiggling your head. One of the labors of Herakles.

## 6

—Sculpture should be a verb not a noun. The *David* is Jack the Giant Killer, handy with strings, so that he can play the harp and have his dark fate in hair, but in his eyes he is the friend of Jonathan, *that sweet rascal from crabstock*, as Grundtvig said. Where Rodin kept going wrong was in sculpting not only nouns but abstract nouns. Nikolai!

—Jo!

—Imagine you can walk on the wind just under the speed of light. There's a magic cunning in your fingers and toes. Fatigue is as unknown to you as to a bee. You have been commanded by the magus Prospero to dart all over an enchanted island to do things impossible for others but easy for you. You have just been given your instructions. The reward of your compliance is freedom. You're about to nip off.

Listening to Prospero, elbows back, chin over shoulder, eyes and mouth wide open, a jump into action, wheeling on toes, and a collision with Samantha who had walked into the studio. A laughing, staggering hug.

—Ariel digging off to execute Prospero's orders.

—Do it again. This time I'll be ready for the hug.

TREE HOUSE

The Korczak group will be this Polish doctor who had an orphanage in the Warsaw ghetto way back when the shitty Germans were burning up all the Jews and there was a day when the Germans took all the kids and Korczak and a woman named Stefa to die at Treblinka, and they all marched through the streets to the cattle cars. I'm to be the boy that carried their flag, the flag of their republic, the orphanage. Gunnar wants you and me to be two pals in the group, arms around each other's shoulders. You'll like Gunnar. He's real. For balls he has a brace of Grade A large goose eggs and a gooseneck of a cock, which his girl Samantha pretends she doesn't go goofy over, I mean all the time he isn't fucking her into fits. She's real, too, and gives me a hard time. Winks at me when I'm posing, and hugs me when we're having a break and stretch. She writes poems and draws posters, and wears badges about Women's Lib. Knows the names of all the butterflies. On his big bulletin board in the studio Gunnar has this list of things Korczak talked to the orphans about every Saturday, or had them swot up, by way of learning about things, famous people like Gregor Mendel and Fabre the bug man, and good and evil, and doing one's duty, and the environment, and how to deal with loneliness, and what sex is, and Samantha has me writing what she calls my responses and ideas, also Gunnar has to write them too, and these go on the bulletin board.

### THE YELLOW OF TIME

In his Roman garden Bertel Thorvaldsen sat reading Anacreon. A basket of Balkan melons, squash, and runner beans sat under the cool of the fig tree, delivered by a girl out of Shakespeare, soon to be carried into the kitchen by Serafina the cook. He had drunk a gourd of well water brought in a stone jug from the country. It tasted of gourd and stone, and of the depths of the earth. Johan Thomas Lundbye's landscape of a Danish meadow hung in his sitting room. There were letters from Copenhagen, Paris, Edinburgh. On his cabinet of Greek, Roman, and Byzantine coins stood branches of oleander in a yellow jug.

### 9

—Morning, halfling. You look tumbled and slept in. It's good you can come early on Saturdays.
—Is there more of that coffee? It was time to get up as soon as I got to sleep.

—Am I to ask intelligent questions or leave your private life private?

Thoughtful grin.

—You probably don't want to know. Mikkel is a maniac and I'm his understudy.

—What about we sit in the sun awhile, with our coffee, in the courtyard. You can skinny down to briefs. Cool air and warm sun, with roses and hollyhocks, lavender and sage, to unsnarl cobwebs from the brain.

—O wow.

—An orange juice and a Vienna bread too?

—Better and better. Gunnar, you're a grown-up Lutheran and all that, but you're a pal, too, aren't you, because the briefs I'm wearing are Mikkel's, or mine and Mikkel's swapped back and forth. Mama makes we wear snow-white underwears here, like I was going to the doctor's, but as I spent the night at Mikkel's, if you're following this.

—Are you embarrassed or bragging? Sounds wonderfully imaginative and comradely to my evil ears.

—Fun. Make Samantha hold her nose. Why evil?

—Evil's a vacuum, they say, where good might be. Nature abhors a vacuum. Therefor nature abhors, and excludes, evil. Grundtviggian logic, wouldn't you say? Being friendly with Mikkel is good sound nature.

—You think?

—I know.

Long silence.

—Nature's good.

—What else could she be?


10


A time machine, H. G. Wells's as modified by Alfred Jarry, made of brass, walnut, and chromium, with manufacturer's plate in enamel on tin. Levers, dials, a gyroscope, all real.

Nikolai, older, in bronze as the pilot. Trim Edwardian clothes, scarf and backward cycling cap.

11

The girl Samantha was like the Modigliani on the big push-pin cork board where forty-eleven postcards, notes, letters, Parisian metro tickets, photographs made a collage for Nikolai to study while he doffed and donned his clothes.
—His mama had, yes, he answered Samantha's question, put it to him, in her arch voice moreover.
—I know mamas, Samantha said with her fetching smile.
—That Gunnar who was at somebody's house where she was, bald brainy people from the university, needed a handsome boy to pose for a statue without a stitch the Georg Brandes Society had commissioned, Ariel he's called, in a play by Vilhelm Shakespeare, and she said she had a rascally son.
—A sensitive son, I imagine she said.
An understanding grin from a crush of soccer jersey pulled up and off.
—Who's just going from cute to goodlooking.
—To adolescent beauty, and who at an astute guess instantly saw in a model's fee skateboards backpacks naughty comicbooks and revolting phonograph records.
On one knee, undoing shoes.
—Ha. What about the score of the first Bach partita, and new fiddle strings, and these new briefs, see.
Gunnar with sharpened chisels.
—I'm getting acquainted, Samantha said, with this Danish angel with the unangelic plumbing fixtures.
—Do angels pee? Are they even oxygen breathers?
—They're all male in Scripture, I believe. But they don't fuck, as each is the only member of a unique species, and species don't crossbreed.
—What a dreary place, heaven.

—I'm not a species, Nikolai said. Gunnar, did you do this man in handcuffs here in the photograph?
—That's Martin Luther King. It's in a church garden over in Jylland, out from Aarhus.

PONIES ON THE FYN

Riding a pony naked through a meadow red with poppies on a sweet day in June, like Carl Nielsen at Østerport (commented on by mallards and green-shanked moorhens as *O a big one with six legs*), Nikolai drank the spring air like a Pawnee and looked for buffalo in the hollows and eagles in the clouds.
—Steady, said Gunnar. You need a break?
—He's miles away, Samantha said. I can see it in his eyes.
—What? Nikolai asked.
—Nikolai's rarely here. He turns up most business-like, sheds his britches, takes his pose, and goes away like Steen to fight the Nazis with the Churchill Gang or in his space pod through phosphorescent interplanetary dust to galaxies with forests of celery and creeping red slime.

13

A session of drawing, Gunnar intent, Nikolai bored, tolerant, behaved.
—Why are grown-ups so dumb?
—Those who are in your words dumb, friend Nikolai, have always been like that. They were dumb children.
      Nikolai thought about this. The silence contained bees, a violin passage of lazy intricacies, a dense stillness.
—On the other hand you have a kind of point. Bright children do grow up to be dull. I wish I knew why. The century's mystery is that intelligent children become teen-age louts, who grow up to be pompous dullards. I'd like to know why.
—Is this a trick question?

—Brancusi at thirty-four had the liveliness to begin to be Brancusi.

—You talk to me as if I were grown up.

—You want me to talk to you as if you were half-witted?

—Only some grown-ups are morons. Most of 'em. You're OK, Gunnar.

—Thanks.

—Tell me more about Korczak, the republic of children, Poland.

## 14

—It's a meadow that shades off into a marsh with reeds and then does sand banks into the cold wet Baltic, out from Hellerup, we can take the train, want to go? You'll turn honey brown.

—Now?

—Just thought of it, so let's do it.

Their locomotive was the Niels Bohr.

—If you thought of this friendly outing, as you call it, when I turned up to pose, how come Edith had a thermos and snack ready in that satchel?

—Those pants, Nikolai. With the obliging fit.

Imp's grin, musing eyes.

—They're this short from the store, and then Mama took in the crotch at the inseam. Packages my mouse neater. If your look means was it her idea, well no. She's so good at sewing that it took her only a minute to do it, and she whistled in a meaningful way while she was clicking it through the sewing machine. A dry cough in the handing over, but never a word. So how come Edith knew you were going to these marshes?

—A meadow all greenest grass and one million wild flowers with a white strand at its foot. A marsh, too, with grebes and mallards.

—How come Edith knew you were going to this midge heaven?

—Second sight. They have it in the Faeroes.

Imp's grin, silly eyes.

Hellerup, a back street, a lane, a field, the meadow sloping down to the strand.

—Drawing block, pencils, sammidges, sunglasses, said Nikolai of the canvas satchel's contents. What's in the thermos?

—A nice couple I know, can't keep their hands off each other, live in that house we passed, in a maze of box hedges. They're now, poor dears, in the United States, at some conference on the economics of cows. This is their property, so we can make ourselves at home.

Curious gaze at Gunnar, a twitched nose, speculative crimping of the corners of the mouth.

—The meadow is a recurring image in Rimbaud. It's his image of the world after the flood. The world anew after being drowned. Shakespeare grew up in meadows, a country boy.

—Rimbaud.

—He called them a harpsichord. The harpsichord of the meadow.

—I like it when you babble, Gunnar. Go back to Rimbaud.

—No underwear.

—And one problem, learn from experience, with abridged and minimized pants is that you can't get them off over your sneakers.

—If you didn't have sneakers the size of boats and socks as thick as towels, you'd have a chance.

—Grown-ups are so fucking tiresome, you know? Who tied these laces? not me. Blue toes and heels to these socks, see.

—Grown-ups know that you take your shoes off before your pants. Rimbaud was a French poet, probably the greatest of our time. He quit writing at 18, became a vagabond.

—I can't wait to have hair all over the top of my feet and toes, like yours. Drives Samantha crazy, I imagine.

Upper lip lifted, Thorvaldsen, eyes dimmed.

—Paisley underwears, what there is of them. Recite me a poem by this Rimbaud.

—Samantha's gift. One has to wear gifts.

> *O saisons, ô chateaux,*
> *Quelle âme est sans défauts?*
> *O saisons, ô châteaux,*
> *J'ai fait la magique étude*
> *Du bonheur, que nul n'élude.*

—Hey! You're beautiful, Gunnar. You've always been big shoulders under a sweater, and raunchy jeans, and forty-four shoes, and underneath you're an Olympic diver.

> I see apples,
> I see pears,
> I see Gunnar's
> Underwears.

Oh seasons, right? Oh chateaux. And something about magic happiness, yuss? This sun's great. I can feel myself turning honey brown.
—What soul is without its faults? I've made a magic study of happiness, or a study of the magic of happiness. Let's look at the marsh.
—Swap dicks with you. Now I see why Samantha drools when she looks at you. Why didn't you bring her, too?
—Two males dressed like Adam are free of the electricity that charges the air when Eve's along.
—I'd be an idiot if I were hung like you.
—It will grow if you drink your buttermilk, eat your spinach, and play with it diligently.

> *O vive lui, chaque fois*
> *Que chante le coq gaulois.*

—There are nests in the marsh grass, grebe or mallard. Every time the French rooster crows cockadoodle, cockadoodle, cockadoodledo!

—Let happiness thrive every time the cock crows. How many times they painted you in the last century, a naked boy on the ocean's edge, Peder Krøyer, Carl Larsson, Anna Ancher, all those masters of tone. The Finn Magnus Enckell. Hammershøi was their Vermeer. There's a charming story of Nexø's about naked spadgers on the beach, somewhere around here.

      Devil dance on shining sand flat.

—How come?

—Symbolism, idealism, Walt Whitman, the Mediterranean past, hope, the beauty of the subject, Thorvaldsen, the Danish heart.

—Did Edith pack any peapods?

      Fingers flipping at mosquitoes, midges, gnats.

—Nietzsche and Georg Brandes. We could go see.

—Hey!

—Walk up.

—I'm too big to ride piggyback, wouldn't you say?

—On my shoulders.

—Ho!

—Ho!

—What's in the thermos is cold milk. Edith thought it the only tipple for a growing Danish boy.

      Fingers wrecking Gunnar's hair.

—I figured you'd go silly.

      Legs out straight, Gunnar holding his shins, Nikolai leaned forward to stare eye to eye upside down.

—Catch! said Nikolai, doubling and pitching forward into Gunnar's arms, deadweight limp, laughing.

—Dig into the satchel and see what Edith calls a picnic. Should I make any remark, however friendly, about the incumbent of the diminished short pants pointing to the sky?

      Downward stare, mock surprise.

—I guess I get a hard on when I'm happy. Sammidges in wax paper. Bananas. Eggs, Vienna breads with raisins and walnuts.

      Brownish pink, stalk and bulb, scrotum round and tight.

      Silly grin, happy eyes.

—It lifts and waggles when you're posing. At your age, it has a mind of its own.

—Yours doesn't? It has my mind, too, sometimes.

—The foreskin slides back, I hope? Some don't.

Foreskin withdrawn from palest violet glans by a ready fist.

—Why don't some don't?

—Why do some people have webbed toes and six fingers? Nature has an awful lot to do in designing a body. She did very well with you.

—This sammidge is country pâté, smells like gym socks worn for two summer weeks, and Gruyère. This one's ham, mayonnaise, and olives.

—One of each. Faeroe Islanders disapprove of choice, on religious principle, I think.

Nikolai among meadow flowers, eating his Vienna bread first.

—Banana next, then sammidges.

—It's a free country.

—Up there, blued out contrary to all you'd think, are the stars, too many to count, in boundless space, and the air that belongs to our planet only, and here at the bottom of the air, us, in a meadow in Denmark, full of wildflowers, ants, microbes, worms, and grass, and under us layers of chalk and clay and solid rock down to we don't know what, but whatever it is, it gets to a center, and starts the other half of a symmetry on out to the other side of the world opposite to where we are now, which is halfway between New Zealand and King Edward VII Land in Antarctica, pods of mooing whales and icebergs with penguins standing around on them gabbling with each other, the *Nautilus* with Kaptajn Nemo playing Buxtehude on his organ, great C-Minor chords thrilling through jellyfish, and then back to us and the mayflies and the grasshoppers, and here we are, Gunnar Rung, playing hookey from chiselling an Ariel out of stone, and Nikolai Bjerg, twelve-year-old Lutheran with his richard stiff.

—You're going to be a poet.

—You did hug me, you know. When Mikkel masturbates, and comes, it's like the white of an egg all over his tummy, maybe two eggs.

—Mikkel's how old?

—Thirteen, but advanced. He says he could come at eleven. This is fun, Gunnar. I should have brought a kite, the breeze is just about perfect. Ouch! Ant on my balls.

—Bring Mikkel around sometimes. Your best friend, is he?

Talking while chewing, eyes closed to think, thumb and fingertips wobbling glans.

—Because.

—When I start the Korczak group, I'll need several kids, girls and boys. You and Mikkel as friends, holding hands, or arms around each other, or somesuch. I want something Korczak would like. He loved his children. I ask you if Mikkel is your best friend, and you answer *because*, which probably isn't bright.

—Good eats, especially as consumed backwards. Actually, these are Mikkel's pants.

15

—The interleaving high outward stretch of the tall oak, Samantha said. That's how this Greek poem begins, by Antiphilos. A good shadower, *euskion*, for *phylassomenois*, people looking for shade, from the ungiving heat of the sun. Its leaves are thicker together than tiles on a roof. And is home to the ringdove, and home to the cricket. And then it says: let me be at home here, too, at perpendicular noon. That's all the poet says, with a hint at the end that he's going to have a nap in the cool shade under the oak.

—There's Holberg's oak over by the old library, Nikolai said, and that sacred oak out in The Hills.

—Don't wiggle, Gunnar said. It's a short poem?

—Six lines, and amounts to a big oak, green and enormous, with pigeons and crickets in it, and an ancient Greek, or Greeks, sitting or lying under it. It makes a lovely poem.

—What's its title? When was it written?
—Greek poems don't have titles. First century, in Byzantium.
The ringdove is a *phatta*, and may be a wood pigeon or the
cushat. In the Bible you get ringdoves in terebinth trees.

Nikolai cooed like a dove and chirped like a cricket.
—You're translating? Gunnar asked.
—Trying to. It seems to be so pure and innocent, yet the oak
was Zeus's tree, and had a dryad in it, a kind of girl Ariel, and
the dove belongs to Aphrodite, and the cricket's squeak and
cluck is a symbol for shepherds letching after each other, or
for the milkmaid with the sunburnt nose and slim bare feet in
the daisies. So what looks like Wordsworth or Boratynski is
actually Sicilian and pastoral, a long time after Theokritos. But
it's looking ahead to nature poetry, if we want to see it that
way, of the kind we begin to get in Ausonius.
—Have I ever heard anyone talk like Samantha? Nikolai asked
the ceiling, crossing his eyes and rounding his tongue like the
bowl of a spoon in his surmising mouth. No, I have never heard
anyone talk like Samantha.
—Break! said Gunnar. Bumpkin has decided to play the village
idiot.
—Let me, Nikolai said pulling on a sweater, see that Greek
poem. What's that word?
—*Branches*.
—And and.
—*Hanging out over spreading oak good shadow high.*
—In Mikkel's tree house there're leaves all around us, even
below, and the light's as green as a salad, and it's cool and
private. Show me the house of the ringdove and cricket.
—*Oikia phatton, oikia tettigon.* House of the ringdove, house
of the cricket. A *tettix* is a cricket.
—Named itself, didn't it?
—*Dendroikia paidon,* tree house for boys.

Golden smile with silver dots for eyes.
—My friend Birgit and I, Samantha said, used to climb out her
bedroom window, in our shimmy tails, into a big tree, I think

it was a very old apple, and sit on limbs, like owls. We thought it a very important thing to do.

### BOY WITH GEESE

In the park, with lakes, in Malmö. Life-size Swedish boy in small britches, three geese, by Thomas Qvarsebo, 1977. Gunnar, Samantha, and Nikolai went over on the boat from Nyhavn to look at it. Nikolai liked the geese, Gunnar the candid modelling, Samantha the big-eared, honest-eyed frankness of the boy.
—And the obviousness, there in the britches, of his being male.
—Wait till you see my and Nikolai's Ariel.
—Sweden, Nikolai said, is Denmark's Lutheran uncle.
—Lutheran aunt, said Samantha.

### BULLETIN BOARD

Red and brown poultry foraging in the high street, and dogs, grass between rocks once squared stone but there is no squared stone in these late days in antiquity, the autumn of an autumn, when portrait statues of the emperors had drilled pucks for eyes, all exactitude lost in swollen bulk, when discernible value was draining from things into money and into a frightened spirituality that hated the body.
—L'Orange, Gunnar said when Samantha asked, *Fra Principat til Dominat*. It happened again in Picasso's sculpture.

### GOLDEN DOVES WITH SILVER DOTS

In the advanced light of a long afternoon, Samantha reading, Gunnar rolling his shoulders, Nikolai rubbing his knees.
—When each of us relates to an idea, separately, essentially, and with passion, we are together in the idea, joined by our differences.
—Kierkegaard, Gunnar said.

Nikolai butted and pushed his way into Gunnar's Icelandic sweater.

—In which, Gunnar remarked to the ceiling, he can pet his mouse, and those of us who are unobservant are none the wiser.

—He's among friends, Samantha said. Each is himself in himself, different. In our separate inwardnesses we keep a chaste bashfulness between person and person that stops a barbarian interference into another's inwardness. Thus individuals never come too close to each other, like animals, precisely because they are united in ideal distance. This unity of differentiation is an accomplished music, as with the instruments in an orchestra.

Nikolai, whistling, came to sit by Samantha and look at the page. She hugged him closer and wrecked his hair.

—He wears your sweater because it's yours.

—Isn't that barbarian, as you've just read us? Not as barbarian as grubbing around down in under the sweater, but then the two would go together, wouldn't they?

—I hope so, Samantha said.

—I don't know what anybody's talking about, Nikolai said.

—Love, I think, Gunnar said. Your namesake Grundtvig wanted everybody to hug and kiss. Kierkegaard, however, saw people in love as two alien worlds circling each other. Grundtvigians went at it along the hedgerow, watched by placid sheep, and in the Lutheran bed, and in the hayloft, but shy Søren was one for guddling down in under a sweater three sizes too large for him, without, I should think, the shameless grin.

—Quit twitting Nikolai, who's looking like the most innocent cherub in God's nursery. Kierkegaard looked like a frog with a sorrow.

—Nikolai Frederik Severin Grundtvig, Nikolai said. Could be I was named for him, do you think?

—You can say you are. We all live in our imagination, don't we? If we don't make ourselves up, others will make up a self for us, and get us to believe it.

Sweet puzzlement in Nikolai's eyes.

—I wonder, Gunnar said, if we don't make everything up? Man, I mean, is a damned strange animal. He lives in his mind. Of course we don't know how animals think, what their opinions are. What does a horse think about all day?

—Maybe, Nikolai said, they just are. Horses and ducks. But, you know, they have lots to pay attention to.

—What you're sculpting, you know, Samantha said over *L'Equipe*, which she had abandoned Kierkegaard for in her nest of cushions by the window, is not really Ariel at all, but Eros, Shakespeare's junior senior giant dwarf Don Cupid.


19

—It can't be done, Nikolai said, but Mikkel brought me piggyback on his skateboard.

—Hello, said Mikkel.

Blond and pink, with awesome blue eyes, Mikkel was dressed in spatter jeans and a sweater from the Faeroes. Fifteen, at a guess. *Dansk fabrikat.* Why did Nikolai say thirteen?

—See, Nikolai said of the stone Ariel, it's me, or will be when it's finished.

—Hey! You're good! Mikkel said to Gunnar, who was edging chisels at the grindstone. I mean, it's tremendous, you know?

—I get paid for posing It's like a job. Are you ready, Gunnar boss man? Is it OK if Mikkel watches? He knows he's to stay out of the way.


20

On Saturdays at the Children's Republic, after their newspaper had been read and the weekly court had tried and fined those charged with bullying, disrespect, hair pulling, disobedience, fibbing, and other high crimes of their little world, Korczak would give a talk. The subject was chosen by the orphans, from a list on the bulletin board, frequently revised.

—So we have put one of those lists on our bulletin board,

Gunnar said, compiled by Samantha from several sources. That's why The Emancipation of Women leads all other topics. —I have not, Samantha said, sticking out her tongue, fiddled with the order.

### 21

Fox bark, gruff. Nikolai monkeyed from the bed to the sill, replying with a cub's whimper. Coupled hand and wrist, Nikolai pulled and Mikkel climbed until he had a kneehold, swinging his other bare brown leg into the room. They sat on the floor, grinning at each other in the dark. They crept like panthers, on fingers and toes, to the bed. Nikolai, naked under the blanket, watched Mikkel tug off his jersey, the tuck of his navel, a dab of shadow on his moonlit front.

In their shy and democratic privacy under the sheets Nikolai speculated on the interestingly different warm and cool places of the body, flinching from cold fingers and toes, the climate of a bed, the frankness of hands. Mikkel whispered that they should suppress talk, as parents can hear better than dogs, and, as Nikolai understood, words are scary and inadequate, things named being compromised thereby, and changed. In the tree house one took off one's pants if the other did, with no more than the complicity of a grin. The gossip of boys is largely fiction, anyway: they enjoyed each other's lies.

#### POLIXENES

We were as twin lambs that did frisk in the sun
And bleat the one at the other.

### 23

Nikolai had just returned from the red plains of Mars. He had parked his space cruiser in a meadow in Iceland, and had a leg-stretching walk through wildflowers and sheep. Then he

transmitted himself through a hyperspace cavity with a swimming roll like that of the bubble in a spirit level, to Copenhagen, where he changed from his mylar-and-platinum anti-
gravity overall into comfortable jeans and jersey. On Strøget
he bought an ice cream and a sack of peapods. As usual, interplanetary travel and ice cream made him amorous, tightened
his balls, and made him importantly happy.

At Gunnar's he entered without knocking, though he
shouted in a breaking treble that he was there.

Silence, but one that had just gone silent.

—Hey! It's me. Ariel. Nikolai.

Thicker silence.

Whispers upstairs.

—O shit, Nikolai said. Look, I'll go away. When should I come
back, huh?

More whispering.

—Come on up, Samantha said. You're friends.

—Better than friends, Gunnar said. You're family.

—I don't want to butt in, Nikolai said with plaintive honesty,
imitating grown-up speech. I can come back.

—You can also come up. We're dressed like Adam and Eve
before they found the apple tree, but then so are you most of
the time you're here.

Nikolai peeked around the bedroom door and lost his
voice.

—The fun's over, Samantha said. Over twice, to brag on Gunnar. We were fiddling around with afterplay and mumbling in
each other's ear.

Gunnar rolled over onto his back, his hands under his
head, the silliest of grins and closed eyes for an expression.
Samantha gathered the eiderdown around her shoulders.

—An American sociologist, she said, would make lots of notes
if I were to say that we have to get dressed so that Nikolai can
take off his clothes to pose.

—Figure and ground, said Gunnar. Or is it context? Maybe just
manners?

He sat up with a yawn and stretch, swinging his legs off the bed.

—A game, he said. I put on my shirt, Nikolai takes his off. I button my top button, you unbutton yours.

—It won't work, Samantha said. You can't put on a sock, or your underbritches, while he takes his off, as there's a shoe intervening, jeans intervening.

—OK, then. Off a shoe and I'll put on a sock.

—Still won't work, Samantha said. Nikolai can't take his jeans off over his shoes.

—Got to pee, said Gunnar.

—Undress, quick quick, Samantha said. Get in the bed.

He untied his shoelaces as if he'd never seen a shoelace before, and his fingers on buttons, belt buckle, and zipper were as strengthless as a baby's. He had just dived under the coverlet Samantha was lifting, in his socks and briefs, heart beating like a chased rabbit's, when Gunnar returned.

—Oh ho! The American sociologist has now walked into a wall.

He took off his shirt, raised the eiderdown, and pulled Nikolai into a hug.

—We still have on our briefs and socks, Samantha said, which I'm now peeling down and off.

A whistle of surprise and compliance from Nikolai.

The only strategy he could think of was to lie on his back with one arm under Samantha's shoulders, the other under Gunnar's. Out of the corners of his eyes he looked in turn at each, for instruction, for a clue. Could they hear his heart thumping? Samantha's breast was cool and warm at once against his ribs. Gunnar's hard freckled shoulder fitted awkwardly under his arm, making it tingle. He kissed Samantha on the cheek, and was kissed back.

—No fair, said Gunnar.

So he kissed Gunnar and was kissed back.

Samantha reached across him to Gunnar, and Gunnar across to Samantha, in some conspiracy of communication, as if words were no longer of any use.

—One big nuzzling rolling hug from each of us, Gunnar said, and we get on with the day. Samantha and Nikolai first, Samantha and me second, Nikolai and me third.

## 24

—Friendly trees, Mikkel said. When Colonel Delgar was turning the dunes and heaths of Jylland back into forests, he found out that if you plant a mountain pine beside a spruce, the two will grow into big healthy trees. Spruce alone wouldn't grow at all. Mycorrhiza in the mountain pine's roots squirt nitrogen and make the spruce happy and tall.

Thick, ribbed, white knee socks, Mikkel's, banded blue and mustard at the top. Shoving them down, his back against Nikolai's shoulder. Flex of pullover hem over pod of his white briefs, hamp of hair tickling the nib of his nose, eyes meeting Nikolai's.

—By 1500 Jylland was a waste heath. Trees are masts. Can you get at the fig newtons? Down in under all the ziplocks they are.

—Friendly trees, Nikolai said, squirming around to work off his shorts. The space, lack of it, in this tree house is friendly. Why are you talking about friendly trees, huh?

Mikkel rocking on his back, wiggling out of his briefs. A smart pubic clump the color of marmalade.

—Fig newtons in one hand, Nikolai said, cock in the other. There are too many legs in this tree house.

Mikkel pulling down Nikolai's briefs.

The two small square windows in Mikkel's tree house looked onto roofs and the skylight onto leaves and branches.

—Gunnar's not *in* this world, Nikolai said. Well, he is and he isn't. To be a sculptor he says you have to read poetry and philosophy and know anatomy like a surgeon and listen to music and go off and be by yourself to make peace with yourself in your soul, and he likes both boys and girls, that's for sure, and is trying to make up his mind which. But he's a good person. Good sculptor. His landlady, the Plymouth Brother from the Faeroes, gets a thrill out of imagining he's a devil, but you can see she likes him, and fusses over him. The looks she gives me when I'm posing.

### 25

The dove in Gunnar's dream flew upside down, carrying a sparrow in its claws.

#### HERAKLEITOS IN THE RIVER

Conventional psychology is misled by a primitive gnostic theory to the effect that things ought normally to appear to sense in their full and exact nature. Nothing could be further from the fact, or more incongruous with animal life and sensibility.

### 27

Gunnar drawing Nikolai's hand.
—King Matt. Tell me more about him.
—In good time. There's a play by Korczak in which children sit in judgment on God and history. Their indictment is almost too terrible to hear. His orphans were for the most children abandoned by their parents and at the mercy of Poland, which is like being a sparrow at the mercy of a hawk.

### 28

Splendid stare of blue eyes.
—Mikkel Angelo made a big buncher statues, yuss, and when was he? I'm so fuckering dumb.
—Last quarter of the 1400s, and sixty-four years into the 1500s. Fingers.
—Eighty fuckering nine years old.
—He was an architect, too, and a painter and a poet.
—David the giant killer.

—Moses with horns.
—The ceiling of the Catholic church in Rome, Italy. Horns?
—Beams of light from his forehead. You shine when you've talked with God. But they look like horns.
—What do you know about sand?
—Sand?
—We're doing sand in school. Geography. It drifts around like oceans. Sloshes. Sand is rock turned to grit by wind and water. Then it packs down again, over a million or so years, and turns back into rock. Crazy.

29

Samantha in a baggy jersey, Gunnar's, looking at drawings of herself. Arrival of Nikolai, pitching his book satchel into a corner.
—Let me see. Hello, Samantha, hello.
—You wore those pants to school?
—Where's Gunnar? Oh, yes. Truly short pants make your legs look longer, you know.
—Having a pee and putting himself back together. We rather got carried away.
—And with these there's no underwear on under, so your nuts and dink can nest in what there is of a pants leg, though they're apt to look out when you're sit, if you're not careful. Tuck back in easy enough.
—Gunnar! Samantha shouted. Come save me, or Nikolai, whichever you think needs protecting from the other.
     Edith looked around the door. Pursed lips.
—Ho! said Gunnar bounding downstairs, zipping up. Flopping wet hair.
—Drawing, drawing! Some days you can, some days you can't. Degas was here, wasn't he? Are you're teasing innocent Nikolai, or is Nikolai trying to see what his charm will get him? A studio's a friendly place.

### 30

A giant land iguana in his silken brown and green network mail, *Conolophus suberistatus* Gray, safe in a convoluted viridity of pisonia, fish fuddle, and guava, trained his red eyes on his cousin amblyrhynchus, changing from voluptuous pink to leaden lava, where red rock crabs grow. And with his eyes on the iguana, Caliban, who has also seen, after the thunder-strokes and howling winds of the tempest, drowned sailors, dropped from the moon, when time was. Their strange clothes are wet and black, rilled in the way of vines about their bony legs and arms, their feet buckled in sodden leather.

### 31

Nikolai danced, a puppet on jerked strings, an eel wiggling, a lunatic hopping, a farmer at Whitsuntide drunk and happy, a Pawnee stomping through the ghost dance, a Christy minstrel balling the jack, a new-hatched devil chasing Lutheran virgins.

Samantha joined him for a Mutt-and-Jeff foxtrot with something Mexican in it. The music was outside, in Gray Brothers. Gunnar and Edith were spreading a board for supper in the courtyard.

—The Lord makes allowances for the young, Edith said. It's a blessing he has on clothes.

### 32

Feeling friendly toward the bobble of red dahlias outside the windows, where the afternoon stood as a tall box of solid and perpendicular light, Nikolai began with a dip to undress. It was a remote out-in-the-country farmyard light, between kitchen and barn, with chickens, a well, old bricks with a felt of moss in corners and under trees. Butterflies, bees, midges.

—Your courtyard is a farm on Fyn, you know? Pushing down

his jeans, he mouthed to the empty air *I am Batman*.

A new book lay on the coffee table, essays on Wittgenstein edited by Jaakko Hintikka.

—Who in private life is a reindeer. It's Wittgenstein you've done a bust of, right? Tall neck and gaze. In a leather jacket with zipper.

Briefs down, he tickled the neb of his penis, a baby's innocence in his smile. The drawing block, colored pencils.

—Today we're drawing. Pull your briefs up, leave your socks on, shirt off. Your hair's a nice muss today. Light's splendid, as you've said. And for reasons I probably oughtn't to pry into, you're sweetly happy, pleased with yourself.

—Happy with just being here, Gunnar. Can I say that? There are lots of good places, the Troll Wood, my room at home, Mikkel's room, the Ny Carlsberg Glyptotek and whichwhat, but this is my best place.


## 33

—We sculptors have no interest in time, and therefore have no language. What we and the critics say about sculpture is usually pig swill.

—Potato peels, mash, and buttermilk, Nikolai said. I've seen it. Tasted it. On a dare from my cousin on the farm. Pigs are delicate eaters, you know.

—Beautiful beasts they are, too.

—Part dog, part hippo.


### KORCZAK TO JOSEF ARNON

Don't you think I look like an old tree filled with children playing like birds in my branches? I'm trying to exclude everything temporal from my thoughts, to relive all that I've ever experienced through the silence within silence.

## 35

Samantha throwing off a shawl and kicking off her shoes.
—Whatever will we do when the Ariel's finished and there's
no Nikolai to do his fetching striptease and be beautiful and
talk nasty?
—I can still drop in, can't I?
—There's the Korczak group, Gunnar said over the whirr of his
grindstone. I have other ideas, too. And then, if I wanted to, I
could be jealous.
   Samantha kissing Nikolai on the mouth.
—I saw that, said Gunnar.
—I'm in love, Nikolai said.

## 36

Having peed shoulder to shoulder at a urinal off The Greening
toward the Fortress, Mikkel and Nikolai grinned at each other
in purest idiocy.
—Some days, Mikkel said, I'm only half horny, you know? As
if I were grown up or there's a hormone short out, but most
days I wake up to a prosperous stiff cock that's going to butt
my fly all day, and hums to itself, and plumps my balls up
tight. Are you like that?
—Worse, I hope.
—Today's a hormone overload. Why do ducks come in threes?
Two drakes and a hen. Is one her spare? Or is one drake the
other's friend?
   They walked, bumping shoulders, up the path behind the
regimental chapel to the ramparts.
—Kierkegaard used to walk here, Nikolai said, round and
around. Gunnar told me that the other afternoon. He said he
only knew me as a kid who turned up on time, posed in the
altogether, jabbered polite and awful nonsense, and went away.
A walk is how you get to know people, he said, and we came
up here. Said he liked the light and the trees and the quiet.
—And Nikolai.

—This is where Niels Bohr's father explained to him how a tree works, photosynthesis and water through the roots and all, and little Niels said, *But, Papa, if it weren't like that it wouldn't be a tree.* Gunnar likes me? Mna. I look like what he thinks Ariel looked like.

### 37

—The Korczak group will be bronze. With rock you have to know exactly what you're shaping, where Nikolai Ariel is inside, which I do, and which I need to get to all at a go.

Gunnar wore sneakers and an American baseball cap only, his naked body powdered over with marble dust.

Industrial yellow-and-blue work gloves, mallet, chisel.

—So your posing is for the finding you in the stone, that's behind us, and for the finishing and smoothing, which begins tomorrow. By tonight it will be here. I got up this morning with it in my eye, in my hands, all the thousand decisions made.

—Golly.

—Golly exactly.

—You want me around? Can I stay and watch?

—Hand me those goggles over there on the shelf. There's going to be dust when I bite into this fucker with the power saw. Samantha's bringing gauze masks, and sandwiches. Edith's away at her sister's. Said something about idols as she left. What she was thinking is that when I'm bringing a work up to the finish line I get raving horny.

—O wow.

—Probably make a little Dane as well as an Ariel, all in a day's work. Get the broom and dustpan and start sacking up the rubble. Into those paper bags it goes, and the bags you put in a neat line in the alley. First, find the wire brush.

Diligence of Nikolai, with stares at Gunnar.

—When did you start, Gunnar? Yesterday the block was my head and shoulders and the outside of my arms and legs, and you were working down the back to my butt. Now about half the rock I was in is on the floor and there're spaces between my arms and body and between my legs, and I can see how the legs are going to be.

—Six this morning. Shooed Edith away around half eight, quoting Scripture. Samantha turned up around nine, made coffee, and got fucked.

—Want me to make more coffee? I get horny, too, posing.

—We can imagine that Shakespeare writing the play, and rehearsing it, and probably acting in it, was not a Lutheran Swede in his great heart.

—First time I was here I went away with balls as tight as a green apple and my handbrother throbbing.

—Goggles. I hear Samantha at the door. And you jacked off twice, panting and mooing.

—Four times. I'm not a baby. Ho, Samantha.

Samantha with her jacket over her head, wet.

—It's raining cats, dogs, and Swedes. The streets are rivers. Nikolai! You count, of course. Gunnar's not in the world when a work fit's on him. When he went full throttle on the Georg Brandes I had to feed him for two days and remind him to pee. Charming reversal: Nikolai practically unrecognizable in clothes, with Gunnar pretty much the way he was born. Reminds me of a horse I saw the other day in the paddock at Rungsted Kyst. He was the only gentleman among mares, and he'd slid out half a metre of pizzle, and was frolicking back and forth, ready for the party, in case anybody invited him.

Ear-to-ear fun, Nikolai's face.

—One foot's here, said Gunnar to himself. The other one's there. Nikolai's going to grit his big square teeth and lay out the sandwiches and make coffee while there's an urgent party upstairs, if some of us take off our knickers.

—Don't have any on.

A sudden hug for Nikolai, and a kiss on the mouth.

—Don't get your feelings hurt. Be brave. Understand. We'll owe you a big favor.

Rain light. The coffee-maker was sort of like the one at home, with cannister and paper filter, reservoir in its back. Should he bolt? He would play it cool. That's how Mikkel would see it through, pants poked out in front and all.

Bedspring music from upstairs, and grunts. A sweet laugh. Swarm of honey in his testicles. We're breathing through our mouth, aren't we, Nikolai, and feeling reckless? We're pouring sugar all over the table, everywhere but in the sugarbowl. We're rattling cups and saucers.

He put the bag of sandwiches on the coffee table. He sat, looking as if he had a folded fish in his pants. He stuck his fingers in his ears, instantly taking them out. This was a learning experience. In Gunnar and Samantha he had people even more understanding than his tolerant, sweet, fussily liberal parents.

He listened to the rain. He composed his account of what was happening, for telling in the tree house.

He was just unbuttoning his pants and easing down the zipper when he heard Gunnar padding downstairs.

—There's beer, he said. I see the coffee making. You're family, I hope you know. Leastways, you are now. O Lord, I didn't even take off my sneakers. There'll be comments made.

—You didn't take off your sneakers, Samantha said coming in wrapped in Gunnar's dressing gown. I'll take over. You've done it all for me, though, sweet Nikolai. I hope you grow up to be a billy goat like Gunnar. It's lots of fun.

—Didn't know I was so hungry, Gunnar said through a mouthful of sandwich. See how the back of the legs echo the whole figure? Nikolai stands as if he were ready to fight the world anyway, but here it's Ariel realizing that if he does what Prospero's ordering, he's free.

Samantha mussed her hand around in Nikolai's hair while reaching for Gunnar's beer to have a sip from.

—Is anybody ever free?

—Only if they want to be. Nikolai's free. How else could he have posed for Ariel?

—Yes, but children don't know they're free, and think of grown-ups as free.

—Am I free? Nikolai asked, munching.

—If you aren't, *lille djævel*, nobody is.

—Two glups of coffee, Gunnar said. Goggles, mallet, chisel.

Nikolai cleaned up, and went back to sweeping dust and marble chips into paper bags. Samantha was curled up in the dressing gown on the couch, having a nap.

Gunnar chiselled, whistled, chiselled. Nikolai watched as intently as if he were doing it himself. The stallion ran around his paddock at Rungsted Kyst, half a metre of pizzle dangling and wagging.

—There is no reality to time at all, you know? None.

Samantha woke with a vague smile.

—I had a wet dream, she said.

—Girls don't *have* wet dreams.

—A lot you know. Complete with orgasm, sweet as jam.

—In that case, Gunnar said, I'll follow you upstairs.

—There's something maybe I ought to tell you, Nikolai said.

—What?

Sigh, bitten lip, silence.

—Nothing, he said.

### THURSDAY

Samantha was on Fyn, visiting her aunt. Gunnar had spent the evening with Hjalmar Johanssen the art critic, who had come to see the finished Ariel. The morning had gone to photographers, the afternoon to Samantha and to seeing her off. And here was Nikolai's knock on the door.

—I've come to spend the night, so you'd better not let me in if you don't want me to. Don't look at me like that.

—Come in, Nikolai. It's late, you know.

—What's that supposed to mean?

—That your parents will be worried you're not home, for one thing.

—Call the Bjergs, if you want to. They'll tell you that Nikolai is in his jammies and fast asleep. Or reading, or watching TV, or whatever he's doing.

—How have you rigged that?

—I haven't. Nikolai has.

—Let me sniff your breath. You're not drunk. Breath's as sweet as a cow's. But obviously I've lost my mind.

—I'm Mikkel. We're best friends, me and Nikolai, tight as ticks. You have only seen Nikolai the one time I brought him around and told you he was Mikkel.

Gunnar sat down and crossed his eyes.

—Go on, he said.

—When Nikolai's mummy asked him if he'd pose for you, the plan fell into place. Nikolai has a girl who has the run of her house every afternoon, and she and Nikolai had already started fucking their brains out when this posing business dropped out of the sky. So I agreed to be him. As I have been. So every afternoon I've been here, he's been coming like a water pistol in the hands of a four-year-old.

—So, hello, Mikkel.

—Hi.

—Now that you've jolted me out of a year's growth, tell me again why you're here. Gently.

—Nikolai wants to pose for the Korczak. As my buddy, arms around each other, on the death march. That will even it all out, right? He got jealous when I told him about how close you and I have become, and about Samantha. The Korczak got through to him. He thought the Ariel old hat. He's the brainy one of us, you know. I've had to pass his parents off as mine. I was sure I'd slip up there. Did I?

—No. Not even with Samantha talking to your, that is, to Nikolai Bjerg's mother fairly often. And I talked with her several times on the phone. Good God! What a talent for the criminal you two little buggers have. You have a career in espionage.

—So here I am.

—And where do your parents think you are?

—I don't have any. I stay with an uncle, who's sort of not all there. The clothes I've worn here were all Nikolai's. I have some of my own now, from my pay from you for posing.

Gunnar speechless for an uncomfortably long time. He went to the front door and locked it.

—Could I have something to eat? Mikkel asked. I can fix it myself.

—Let's fix something together. Ham and eggs, toast and jelly. Tall cold glasses of milk. But come upstairs first. Let's make you feel at home.

—Gunnar.

—Right here, Mikkel. I'll have to practise. Mikkel, Mikkel.

—Are we friends?

—Friends.

Big crushing hug.

—Sit on the bed. I've watched you undressing so many times, and now I'm going to do it, starting with these knotted laces which surely Nikolai tied, not you. Socks that smell of dough. Stand up. Now we unbutton one shirt with a whiff of vinegar underarm. Scout belt. Slides right through, right? Zipper. And by the God of the Lutherans, you're liking this. Pants and nice briefs down and off. Now you're in Nikolai's work clothes, but you've changed from Nikolai to Mikkel, with Shakespeare grinning down from heaven, don't you imagine? So I'm seeing Mikkel stitchless for the first time. But as it's chilly, let's, if I can find it, here we go, put this on you.

—Sweat shirt. Royal Academy of Art. Golly.

—Sort of covers your butt halfway to the back of the knees and swallows your hands. Here, let's add the American baseball cap and have our eats.

—Gunnar.

—Mikkel.

### 39

The high fields of Olympos. Yellow sedge in a meadow. Sharp blue peaks beyond, seamed with snow. The eagle sank out of the cold sky and set him in the field of yellow sedge.

But there was no eagle when he turned, heart still thumping so hard that he had to breathe through his mouth, only a man.

—So, said the man, in a splendid Greek that was neither of the farm or the city, we are here.

—Where be the eagle, Mister Person? It clutched onto me and grabbed me up away from my sheep, and carried me through the air. Closed my eyes, peed and prayed. Where be we?

—On Olympos, that great place. We walk over that knoll yonder and into the palace that rules the world, save for some infringements by fate and necessity, love and time, which are tyrants over us all. Everything that's evil comes from the north. But in the south of time I am king.

—Never been so mixed up in all my life. How do I git home from here, Mister Person? 'Cause that's all I aim to do: git home, and fast.

—You will not age here, and when you go home your sheep will not have noticed you've been gone. I can splice time onto time, with a bolt or two of eternity.

—Shit!

—You need not even imagine that you are here, now. Because on Olympos there is neither here nor now. You are so many words written by a polished writer named Loukianos, of Samosata in Kommagene, who will live two millennia from now. Look you, here before the gate, these are friendly trees. The one will not grow without the other.

The curving street inside the gate (it opened of itself) was paved with stones laid down when Ilion was a forest. They walked along narrow paths among trees which the boy Ganymed could not name until they arrived at a building with cyclopean rock fitted together in irregular hexagons.

—It sure is foreign here, Mister.

—A sweet soul, Loukianos. There was a time when he was an Aethiopian named Aisopos, who understood the speech of animals.

—I can talk sheep. *Baa baa.*

Later, when Zeus had shown Ganymed to some very strange people, a nice lady who only looked at him briefly from her loom, a fat lady who sniffed, a handsome gentleman writing music and couldn't be bothered to look, an amiable red-faced blacksmith who squeezed his arm, and lots of others. At a long family table with buzzing talk, Zeus lifted him onto his lap and said that after so exciting a day they were going to bed, together.

—Don't recommend it, said Ganymed. I sleep with Papa at home, and he says that I twist and turn all night, and talk in my sleep, and that my knees and elbows are as sharp as stakes.

—I will not mind.

—Besides, I want to sleep with that fellow down there, name of Eros, your grandson. He's neat.

Whereupon the fat lady laughed so hard that she had to be helped from the table.

## 40

Sunlight through sheets. Twenty toes. The phone.

—Accept a call from the Fyn? Oh yes. Hello, hello! Yes, I'm probably awake. Nikolai's here in the bed with me. Well, he spent the night. Listen carefully. He's not Nikolai and never has been. He stood in for Nikolai, who was having some kind of torrid affair with a bint, while his adoring trusting parents thought he was being an Ariel for Denmark's most promising young sculptor. He's Mikkel, the friend Nikolai talked about so much, I mean of course the Mikkel Mikkel talked about so much. Don't scream into the phone: it bites my ear. No, I'm not drunk and I haven't lost my mind. You should see him. Mikkel, that is. We've only seen him charmingly nude. Now he's decidedly naked, and his hair looks like a cassowary. Oh yes, you know what boys are like. Disgraceful, yes, and frowned on by psychologists and the police, but lots of fun. The clergy are of two minds about it, I believe. Actually, he went to sleep while we were talking about how friendly it was sharing a bed. I'm putting him on the thread.

A good cough, first.

—'lo, Samantha. I'm not as awake as Gunnar. Congrats on

being pregnant. Gunnar told me last night. You must show me
how to change diapers and dust on baby powder. None of last
night happened, you know? Yes, I'm Mikkel.

Listening, head cocked, tongue over lips.

—And I'll give you a big hug, too, when you get back. Tuesday?
OK, here's Gunnar again.

By way of good manners, Mikkel rolled out of bed. Downstairs he started coffee and poured orange juice into burgundy
glasses, for style. The studio seemed strange, and he looked at
the rosy marble of the Ariel as if he'd never seen it before.

# *And*

A papyrus fragment of a gospel written in the first century shows us Jesus on the bank of the Jordan with people around him. The fragment is torn and hard to read.

In the first line Jesus is talking but we cannot make out what he's saying: too many letters are missing from too many words to conjecture a restoration. It's as if we were too far back to hear well.

We catch some words. He is saying something about putting things in a dark and secret place. He says something about weighing things that are weightless.

The people who can hear him are puzzled and look to each other, some with apologetic smiles, for help in understanding.

Then Jesus, also smiling, steps to the very edge of the river, as if to show them something. He leans over the river, one arm reaching out. His cupped hand is full of seeds. They had not noticed a handful of seeds before.

He throws the seeds into the river.

Trees, first as sprouts, then as seedlings, then as trees fully grown, grew in the river as quickly as one heartbeat follows another. And as soon as they were there they began to move downstream with the current, and were suddenly hung with fruit, quinces, figs, apples, and pears.

That is all that's on the fragment.

We follow awhile in our imagination: the people running to keep up with the trees, as in a dream. Did the trees sink into the river? Did they flow out of sight, around a bend?

# The Lavender Fields of Apta Julia

There is no such thing as time on a summer afternoon. The green and blue of the lavender fields, the tumbled clouds over the pine wood, the Roman bridge neither slide along the river of time nor feel its current pass through them.

—It's the drone of the bees, Julie said, stops time. And the fragrance of the lavender drenches it, and puts it to sleep.

They had built their boxcar beyond the lavender fields where the woods begin.

—Raise sweet children, bright children, Anne-Marie said in her grandmother's raspy voice, and what do they do? They build a boxcar.

—Well, Grandma, Bernard said with tenor innocence, it's to play in.

—It's not being able to keep an eye on us that bugs them.

Julie, Bernard, Anne-Marie, and Marc built their boxcar beyond the lavender fields where the woods begin. Five metres long, two wide, it sat knee-high above the pine-needle floor of the wood on corner posts braced with diagonal studs.

—A shoebox to the power of fifteen, Marc said, with doors in the middle. It has the feel of a real boxcar. The doors are sort of permanently open.

—Boxcar doors are sometimes open, Anne-Marie said, sometimes closed, even when the train's moving. We got the proportions right.

Knocking apart the packing crates salvaged from back of the factory had been as much fun as building the boxcar: floor, walls, top, pie-pan brake wheels, the ladder up.

The light in the boxcar was neither room light nor tent

light. At the doors the light was that of the wood. The dark ends of the inside were brightened by small high windows.

—Ours, Julie said, patting her knees, all ours.

—Lavender fields out one door, the wood out the other, Marc said. It's a tree house that's a boxcar. Along the river, on the tracks, in all kinds of weather. Let's all hug.

—*The Autumn Crocuses*, Julie announced.

Marc sighed, crossed his eyes, and twiddled his fingers.

—*The meadow is splendid and lethal in autumn the cows grazing there are placidly poisoning themselves.*

—Apollinaire.

—Anne-Marie's underpants are a meadow, Bernard said, what there is of them, cornflowers, buttercups, daisies.

—*Crocuses the lilac of a black eye.*

Bernard had entered the boxcar with high elbows and a bound. He lay on his side in the straw, hands under his cheek, eyes alert.

A bird whistled a trill, went silent, and began again with dotted notes and sharp rests, like a dripping faucet, before another trill.

There was a distant dry rasp of crickets.

He had known where Honduras was in class. And M. Brun had said that General de Gaulle had never talked over the telephone.

A sulphur butterfly flew at changing heights through the doors of the boxcar, from the lavender fields to the wood.

—*Your eyes are like these flowers, violet and dark as autumn. They poison me as the crocuses poison the cows.*

—Poor sick cows.

—M. Brun explained why the crocuses are like mothers who are daughters of their daughters and if Apollinaire had any more punctuation than Marc has hair in his britches you could follow him better.

—The crocus blooms before it has any leaves. There's an article on it in the *Encyclopedia* under *Sons before Fathers*.

—*School children come in a fracas elves in winter jackets with hoods playing harmonicas and pick crocuses mothers that are daughters of daughters and are the color of your eyelids.*

Anne-Marie began a dance to the poetry.

Bernard pretended to be asleep.

A Roman cart drawn by two white oxen crossed the stone bridge.

Marc was General de Gaulle refusing to talk over the telephone, batting at gnats.

—*The children bob like flowers in a demented wind.*

—*The cowherd sings*, Anne-Marie joined in.

—*And the cows*, they recited together, *abandon forever, mooing and shambling slow, this autumn meadow beautiful with deadly flowers.*

Marc grunted.

Beyond a march of sunflowers, laundry on a line, fragrant with lavender, Marc recognized his summer shirts, socks, underpants, jeans. Sunflowers like Aztec kings in green mantles.

The abrupt bluff. The stone bridge, over which the Romans passed in carts laden with sacks of lavender.

Apta Julia in Provincia Gallia.

And in the river, once, in the time of the painters of Lascaux, seals. Back when trees walked, owls spoke oracles, and the moon gave signs.

—Wolves, Marc said, at the dark of the moon.

—We could make a film here, Anne-Marie said. A shoebox on a tripod, with round candy boxes for the Michel Mouse ears on top. Lights, and the little board with a hinged stick that snaps at Lights! Camera! Action!

—Better than reciting poetry, that's for sure.

—A film about Russians on the way to Siberia. Overheard saying that Stalin's feet stink.

—The tundra, gray and brown. A hundred kilometres and nothing but the flat tundra.

—With warps and waves in it. A long shot with our train as

small as a string sliding along.

—Or we could bring in the cow, dogs, and cats, and be Noah's ark.

—Jews on the way to Drancy. We could escape. Pig-eyed Nazis shooting at us.

—Time to kiss, Julie said.

Bernard began searching in his pockets.

—Licorice, he said. They're the best. Besides, Julie likes 'em too.

—Better than yesterday's lime.

—I think I'll climb the pine tree, Marc said. All the way to the top today. Off your shoes, Anne-Marie, and come up after me, bet you won't.

—Bet I will.

Bernard pinched a licorice pastille from its box with a shepherd and shepherdess pictured on it in eighteenth-century rustic finery, with laundered sheep watching in innocent wonderment as the seated shepherdess accepts a pastille from the standing shepherd. Bernard nevertheless put the pastille in his own mouth. Other times, other manners.

Marc, shinnying up the pine barefoot, said over his shoulder to Anne-Marie, hair flopping across his eyes, this is the first good hold. It's easy. Then, watch me, you go around to the other side, holding on good. The next best hold is right there, see? I'll wait until you're on the limb I've just left, so we'll be together all the way up.

Anne-Marie, untying her shoes and watching Julie and Bernard begin their long kiss, passing the pastille back and forth in their mouths, monkeyed up the limb Marc had climbed beyond.

—Don't look down, Marc said. You'll get swimmy-headed.

Julie and Bernard, hugging, sank to their knees in a slow topple sideways.

—They're going to kiss lying down. We're going to kiss when we get down, huh?

—It gets easier as you come up. The limbs are closer. I can see the barn and the horses.

—I can see your underpants real good.

—Don't go to any limb I haven't been on. If it holds me, it'll hold you. What does kissing get us?

—They're playing footsie. I can only see their sneakers from here.

—Why did Julie recite that poem by Apollinaire? Guillaume. He was in Grandpa's war, with the Boches, the tanks, and the trenches. Wore a big bandage on his head.

—We had to learn it for Ma'mselle Trudeau. He had a girlfriend named Annie, who moved to Texas and became a Mennonite.

—What's that?

—Some species of the *culte baptiste*. We could gross out Julie and Bernard by throwing our clothes down from the top of the tree.

—Crazy. Would they notice?

—In time. They can't kiss forever.

—I can see the top of the bluff. Old Barzac and his donkey are on the ridge road, loading up with firewood. Higher, and you can see the shine on the river bend, like silver.

—I think I'm ruining my knees.

—Keep your legs stiff. Don't try to climb with 'em. Climb with hands and feet, like me. Watch.

—Our tarpaper roof on the boxcar is practically covered with pine-needles, like the thatched houses up north.

—There's a squirrel watching us, over in the next tree. We had to learn a poem by Jules Supervielle, about a math class, with a triangle and circle on the blackboard, and how an angle looked like a wolf's mouth. We're better than halfway up. When do we start being Tarzan and Jane?

—We've done that Supervielle too. He's from Uruguay. I like his poem about the creation of the world. God has the mountains moving around, which he decides won't do, and makes them stand still. Marc, are you feeling this tree sway, or am I getting dizzy?

—It's swaying a little. The branches up here are stronger. They're newer.

—The lavender's lovely from this height. Hallo, you've got a seat across two limbs.

—See how I've got my ankles locked around each other? I'm offing my *maillot* here. I'll have to throw it wide, or it'll catch on a limb. I don't think we *can* shed our togs by throwing them one at a time. We'd never get 'em out of the limbs. Come on up. I see another seat just there. I'll show you what we can do.
—*D'accord*, but what?
—Once we're bare-assed, we make a bundle, all knotted together, of both our togs, and that'll have the weight to be chucked clear, out, over, and down. I'll kiss you at the top, or as high as we can go. Tie your *maillot* around your neck. Pull off your shorts and underpants together.
—I'm getting dizzier.
—Quit looking down.
—My knees and elbows have turned to water.
—Come up here. I'll slide around to the other side.
—I think I can. You're naked.
—Nothing to it. Hug the trunk, and I'll get your things off for you. Bernard and Julie are probably feeling pretty good about now, wouldn't you say? They got a little wild yesterday with their hands when they'd had their tongues in each other's mouths, icky, for what seemed like an hour but was really, what, twenty minutes? I'll have to hold my clothes in my teeth till I get you buff. Have you got a good hold?
—I'll stare at your peter. Let me do the button and all you have to do is pull. What? Oh, lift my foot, got you.

Holding all their clothes in a wad against his chest, Marc said:
—OK now, hold me around the waist, hugging me and the tree together, and I'll knot everything in my *maillot*, and pitch it down. There!
—Did it clear? I couldn't look.
—I can't see where it went. Sit down across the limbs you're standing on, or do you want to climb higher? I can. I've got a good hold on you. You can't fall.
—I'll go as high as you want. I feel weightless, you know, and strange.
—Lean around for a kiss.

—Open mouth, like Bernard and Julie?

They slid jutted tongues into mouths as wide as nestling birds, Marc's eyes crossed for comedy to help his blush. He kneaded Anne-Marie's shoulder blades. She held the back of his neck, for dear life and affection together. The kiss was experimental and brief.

—Hallo.

—Hallo!

—Two limbs higher, Marc said. We'll have a view to take your breath away.

—Your peter's up.

—It was your idea that we show all. Haven't you seen one before?

—Does it feel good? Yours is the first. You're as red as a tomato. I mean I've not seen one up before. Your balls are as pinky purple as a pomegranate.

—Two limbs higher, come on. By the good God, you can see the horizon all the way around up here.

—Can I get on the same limb with you? You can hold me around the waist.

—As long as we're trading secrets, we are, aren't we, I didn't know that girls had such a big notch.

—I know two girls my age who have hair already. I'm slow, I guess.

—Does Julie?

—No. Can I feel your peter? I mean, put my fingers around it.

—I guess so. I mean, sure, Anne-Marie.

—Marc.

—Pull its hood back, Anne-Marie.

—*Le prépuce.* It slides easy. Does it hurt, pulled back, I mean?

—Does chocolate cake with Chantilly cream taste good? Hold tight for another kiss. Slide it up, and back.

—And only God seeing us.

—And some interested angels, I hope. Can I touch, too? I know there's a place. Anne-Marie.

—Marc, cher Marc. Here.

Bernard's voice, from below:

—Anne-Marie! Marc! We heard something drop, and we looked all around, our hearts stopped, till we found your duds in a bundle. You're up there? Where? Don't scare us like this!

—At the very top! can't you see us?

—*Merde*. At the fucking *top* of which tree?

—The one you're under. Look up. We're Adam and Eve by way of dress.

—Anne-Marie! Julie called. Marc! You're shameless! A scandal! Who would have believed it?

—We're OK up here, Marc hollered down. Go on with your smooching. There are lots of pastilles left.

—Come down! It's dangerous to be that high.

—Go wiggle your toes.

—We may stay up here for an hour or so, Anne-Marie called down. If I lose my hold, I'll float around awhile before drifting to the ground.

—What if somebody comes?

—They won't look up. Can *you* see us?

—Barely.

—I can't, Julie said. Show me where.

—What are you doing?

—Guess.

They were in the tree half an hour. At one point Bernard climbed halfway up, and was shooed down. Marc first, Anne-Marie right above him, they climbed down, whistling in duet Colonel Bogey's March.

On the ground, Marc said:

—Step onto my back, and jump.

Which Anne-Marie did.

They stood grinning, arms around each other's waists. Julie pretended to be shocked, and hid her eyes. Bernard divided his inspection between the two, for information. They were speckled over with sprits of pine bark.

—Have a good snuggle? Marc asked. Where's our bundle?

Julie fetched it from the boxcar, and tossed it to Anne-Marie.

The next afternoon, the summer keeping its blue sky, after Julie had helped her mother shell peas and hang out a wash, after Anne-Marie and Marc had been into Apt with Marc's mother to price school clothes on sale, and after Bernard had bicycled to the parsonage to pick up and deliver his share of the parish magazine, a chore farmed out among his scout troop, they each went by a different and deceptive way to their boxcar in the pinewood.

Bernard, the first to arrive, had washed his wheat-blond hair, and studied himself in the mirror for longer than ever in his life, except to make monster faces. He chinned himself ten times on the boxcar door before he realized that he was making his armpits smelly, quit, sat and cupped his hand over his crotch, shuffled his sneakers in pine needles, untied them and promptly tied them again. A billow of white clouds was piling up over the lavender fields from the east. He turned quickly. Marc was behind him, through the other door.

—Boy! are you sneaky!

—Wanted to see if I could slip up on you. Where are we all?

—A matter of who gets away when.

Bernard slipped his hand down into his pants.

—Like that, huh?

—It's awful.

—Whatever you're scheming won't happen. It never does. Going up the tree just happened. I couldn't have planned it in a hundred years. I see Julie coming through the lavender.

Big smile, and a skip in her walk.

She sat beside Bernard, hugged him around the shoulders, and kissed him on the cheek.

A bird whistled a trill, was silent, and began again with dotted notes and sharp rests, like a dripping faucet, before another trill.

Dry rasp of crickets.

—I didn't, Bernard said, know where Honduras was in class. Put my underwear on inside out this morning.

—Are we different? Julie asked.

Bernard lay back, fainting, his arms as far back as he
could reach, legs straight up, pigeon-toed, eyes wide open,
dead. Julie traced a circle around his navel with a compass of
finger and thumb.

—Where *is* Honduras? Marc asked, picking at his shoe laces.

Julie, watching a ride of midges and a turn of motes in the
diagonal shaft of light between the doors of their boxcar while
teasing the tongue of Bernard's belt from its buckle, said that
Honduras, full of parrots and Mayan ruins in its jungles, was
one of the jigsaw countries in *l'Amérique Centrale.*

—Other people in other places, Marc said, are instructive to
think about, as there are millions of them all doing something,
the Chinese up to their knees in rice paddies reading Mao, Mon-
golians in ear-flaps riding yaks, and so on, with never a thought
about us way on the other side of the lavender field, inside the
pinewood, in the wilds of France, minding our own business.

—Like, Bernard said from his collapse, fallen from the sky,
saying poems. Everybody listen.

> *Sur le chemin de Saint-Germain*
> *J'ai rencontré trois petits lapins*
> *J'en mets un dans mon armoire*
> *Il me dit: il y fait trop noir*
> *J'en mets un dans mon pantalon*
> *Il me suce mon p'tit crayon*
> *J'en mets un dans ma culotte*
> *Il me ronge ma petite carotte*

—That's vulgar, Marc said after a silence in which they could
hear through the cricket racket somebody approaching.

Anne-Marie.

—I saw a lizard on the Roman wall, she said. He let me look
at him for two seconds. And there's a stand of blue chicory
just before you get to the old pear tree, as pretty as Monet.
What was Bernard's poem about, sucking pastilles *à deux*?

—Nothing so refined, but sort of, Julie said.

Bernard fished around in his pockets. Pastilles.

Anne-Marie flopped down beside Marc. Grinning stare, eyes laughing.

—Progress, Bernard said, is what we made yesterday. Never look back.

—Zipper's stuck, said Julie, tugging.

Bernard propped on his elbows, watching.

—Pull up again, and then down. Not that I believe this.

—I had this feeling that the lizard had been there a thousand years, since Apta Julia of the Romans. Their bridge is still here, and their walls. French is just old, old Latin, and what if some of their gods that they brought with them are still around? Between the lavender fields and the hills they'd be, left behind.

—Anne-Marie's gaga, Bernard said, and whimpered. The pastilles are black currant. Pinch one out. Are Anne-Marie and Marc going up their pine?

—That was because Marc was bashful.

—Showing off, you mean.

—We're friends together, aren't we?

—Friends, said Marc.

—Friends, said Julie.

—Friends, said Anne-Marie.

—Friends, said Bernard.

Lavender is one of the verticillate plants whose flower consists of one leaf divided into two lips, the upper lip, standing upright, is roundish, and, for the most part, bifid; but the under lip is cut into three segments which are almost equal: these flowers are disposed in whorls, and are collected into a slender spike upon the top of the stalks. The whole lavender plant has a highly aromatic smell and taste, and is famous as a cephalic, nervous, and uterine medicine.

Theophrastos in his *Plants* places lavender (*Lavandula spica*) or, as his Greek is, *íphyon*, among the summer garland flowers, along with rose campion, the *krinon* lily, and sweet marjoram from Phrygia. He also mentions it as a flower that must be grown from seed.

Vergil in the second eclogue of his *Bucolics* puts lavender along with hyacinth and marigold among the aromatic herbs, and in his *Georgics* with thyme as forage for bees and a flavor for honey. John Gerard wrote in *The Herball or General Historie of Plants* (1597) that lavander spike hath many stiffe branches of a wooddy substance, growing up in the manner of a shrub, set with many long hoarie leaves, by couples for the most part, of a strong smell, and yet pleasant enough to such as do love strong savors. The floures grow at the top of the branches, spike fashion, of a blew colour. The distilled water of Lavander smelt unto, or the temples and forehead bathed therewith, is a refreshing to them that have the catalepsy, a light migram, and to them that have the falling sicknesse, and that use to swoune much.

The floures of Lavander picked from the knaps, I meane the blew part and not the husk, mixed with cinnamon, nutmegs & cloves, made into a pouder, and given to drink in the distilled water thereof, doth helpe the panting and passion of the heart, prevaileth against giddinesse, turning, or swimming of the brain.

John Parkinson in his *A Garden of Pleasant Flowers* (1629) says that Lavender groweth in Spain aboundantly, in many places so wilde, and little regarded, that many have gone, and abiden there to distill the oyle thereof whereof great quantity now commeth over from thense unto us: and also in Lanquedocke, and Provence in France.

# The Kitchen Chair

It was a breathless, gray day, leaving the golden woods of autumn quiet in their own tranquillity, stately and beautiful in their decaying, an afternoon soon after she had moved into a cottage at Grasmere to keep house for her brother William. She had brought a kitchen chair and a milking stool out into the fine weather, to write in her journal. There would be, in time, a garden where she sat, the public road to her left, the yellowing woods to her right. Tucking back a strayed strand of hair around her ear, opening her journal on her lap, she wrote: *It is a breathless, grey day, that leaves the golden woods of autumn quiet in their own tranquillity, stately and beautiful in their decaying.*

Johnson preferred *gray*; William, *grey*.

As in Horace, the words are in an order but are free to form associations of their own. *Leaves*, a verb, easily becomes a noun and takes up with *golden*, for golden leaves are what she's looking at. Leaves in the underworld are of gold, where the vegetation is all of metal, with mineral and crystal flowers. Autumn is Proserpina's return to the realm of artifice, where lifeless stone and iron pretend to be apple and pear. Autumnal decay is nature's grief over her departure.

Until she wrote *autumn*, her sentence was in English. Then Latin began to sift in: *quiet* and its cousin *tranquillity*, as if the older language had the power to cast a spell on us when we write. *Decaying*, she knew, meant falling, and thus she can entwine two roots and tie in the English *fall* under *autumn*. She cannot keep *decay* from meaning *rot*. *Standing* lies encoded in *stately*. The trees stand on their estate. Caesar (she imagines him on a horse) brought *bella* into Gaul. When the Norse king William brought it to Hastings, it had become *beau*, and to its noun *beauté* we English added the *full*.

*Breathless* is an apt word, even though it means both a stillness of wind on such a calm day as this, beautiful and voluptuously calm, and not breathing, as in death. With both meanings was Proserpina familiar.

Gray is a deathly color, and yet it is clouds, which are water, high and cold, the source of life, that grizzle the sky.

It is a breathless, gray day, that leaves the golden fall woods unanswering in their own stillness, kingly and comely in their dying.

# The Concord Sonata

### AN AUTUMN AFTERNOON

At his small sanded white pine table in his cabin at Walden
Pond on which he kept an arrowhead, an oak leaf, and an *Iliad*
in Greek, Henry David Thoreau worked on two books at once.
In one, *A Week on the Concord and Merrimac Rivers,* he wrote:
Give me a sentence which no intelligence can understand. In
the other, *Walden, or Life in the Woods,* he wrote three such
sentences, a paragraph which no intelligence can understand:
I long ago lost a hound, a bay horse, and a turtledove, and am
still on their trail. Many are the travellers whom I have spoken
concerning them, describing their tracks and what calls they
answered to. I have met one or two who had heard the hound,
and the tramp of the horse, and even seen the dove disappear
behind a cloud, and they seemed as anxious to recover them as
if they had lost them themselves.

### JOHN BURROUGHS

Thoreau did not love Nature for her own sake, or the bird and
the flower for their own sakes, or with an unmixed and disin-
terested love, as Gilbert White did, for instance, but for what
he could make out of them. He says: The ultimate expression
or fruit of any created thing is a fine effluence which only the
most ingenuous worshiper perceives at a reverent distance
from its surface even. This *fine effluence* he was always reaching after, and often grasping or inhaling. This is the mythical
hound and horse and turtledove which he says in *Walden* he

long ago lost, and has been on their trail ever since. He never abandons the search, and in every woodchuck hole or muskrat den, in retreat of bird, or squirrel, or mouse, or fox that he pries into, in every walk and expedition to the fields or swamps or to distant woods, in every spring note and call that he listens to so patiently, he hopes to get some clew to his lost treasures, to the effluence that so provokingly eludes him.

This search of his for the transcendental, the unfindable, the wild that will not be caught, he has set forth in this beautiful parable in *Walden*.

### GEESE

Well now, that Henry. Thursday one of the Hosmer boys told him he'd heard geese. He wants to know everything anybody can tell him in the way of a bird or skunk or weed or a new turn to the wind. Well, Henry knew damned good and well that it's no time to be hearing geese. So, always assuming his leg wasn't being pulled, he sat down and thought about it. And after awhile, didn't take him long, he got up and walked to the station. He didn't ask. He told Ned that at half past one on Thursday a train had passed through with a crate of geese in the baggage car. That's a fact, Ned said, but I don't recollect anybody being around here at the time.

### STANLEY CAVELL

I have no new proposal to offer about the literary or biographical source of these symbols in perhaps his most famously cryptic passage. But the very fact that they are symbols, and function within a little myth, seems to me to tell us what we need to know. The writer comes to us from a sense of loss; the myth does not contain more than symbols because it is no set of desired things he has lost, but a connection with things, the track of desire itself.

## THE JOURNAL: 1 APRIL 1860

The fruit of a thinker is sentences: statements or opinions. He seeks to affirm something as true. I am surprised that my affirmations or utterances come to me ready-made, not fore-thought, so that I occasionally wake in the night simply to let fall ripe a statement which I never consciously considered before, and as surprisingly novel and agreeable to me as anything can be.

### 6

And yet we did unbend so far as to let our guns speak for us, when at length we had swept out of sight, and thus left the woods to ring again with their echoes; and it may be many russet-clad children, lurking in those broad meadows with the bittern and the woodcock and the rail, though wholly concealed by brakes and hardhack and meadowsweet, heard our salute that afternoon.

### 7

Solitude, reform, and silence.

### 8

In *A Week on the Concord and Merrimac Rivers* Thoreau wrote: Mencius says: If one loses a fowl or a dog, he knows well how to seek them again; if one loses the sentiments of the heart, he does not know how to seek them again. The duties of all practical philosophy consist only in seeking after the sentiments of the heart which we have lost; that is all.

9

Duke Hsuan of Qi arranged his skirts and assumed a serene face to receive the philosopher Meng Tze, and who knows how many devils had come with him? The magicians had drilled the air around the gates with incessant drumming, and the butlers were burning incense.

The duke could see wagons of millet on the yellow road. The philosopher had apparently travelled in some humble manner. From the terrace he could see no caravan. There was no commotion among the palace guard.

Sparrows picked among the rocks below the bamboo grove.

A merchant was handing in a skip of persimmons and a string of carp at the porter's lodge. The weather was dry.

The philosopher when he was ushered in was indeed humble. His clothes were coarse but neat, and his sleeves were modest. He wore a scholar's cap with ear flaps.

They met as gentlemen skilled in deference and courtly manners, bow for bow. The duke soon turned their talk to this feudal baron or that, angling for news. There had for years been one war after another.

—And yet, Meng Tze said, the benevolent have no enemies.

Duke Hsuan smiled. Philosophers were always saying idiotic things like this.

—The grass, Meng Tze continued, stands dry and ungrowing in the seventh month and the eighth. Then clouds darken the sky. Rain falls in torrents. The grass, the millet, the buckwheat, the barley turns green again, and grows anew. Nothing we are capable of can control this process of nature. And yet men who ought to be the caretakers of other men kill them instead. They are pleased to kill. If there were a ruler who did not love war, his people would look at him with longing, loving eyes. It is in nature to love the benevolent.

So there was to be no gossip about Hwan of Ch'i, or Wan

of Tsin. So the duke asked politely:

—How may a ruler attain and express benevolence?

—He should regard his people as his charges and not with contempt.

—Am I one, the duke asked slyly, who might be so benevolent?

—Yes.

—How?

—Let me tell you about a duke. I had this from Hu Ho. A duke was sitting in his hall when he saw a man leading an ox through the door. The duke asked why, and was told that the ox was to be slaughtered to anoint a ceremonial bell with its blood. Just so, said the duke, but don't do it. I cannot bear the fear of death in its eyes. Kill a sheep instead.

—This is a thing I did, the duke replied. You have learned of things in my court.

—Yes, Meng Tze said with a smile. And I see hope for you in it. It was not the ox but your heart you were sparing.

—The people thought otherwise. They said I begrudged an ox. Qi is but a small dukedom, but I can afford the sacrifice of an ox. It had such innocent eyes and it did not want to die.

—And yet you sent for a sheep. You knew the pity you felt for the ox. How was the sheep different?

—You make a point, the duke said. You show me that I scarcely know my own mind.

—The minds of others, rather.

—Yes. You are searching for compassion in me, aren't you? In *The Book of the Odes* it is written *the minds of others I am able by reflection to measure*. You have seen why I spared the ox and was indifferent to the misery of the sheep. I did not know my own mind.

—If, Meng Tze said with great politeness, you will allow me to play that lute there by the bronze and jade vessels, I will sing one of the most archaic of the odes, as part of our discourse.

The duke with correct deference asked him by all means to sing it.

Meng Tze, finding the pitch, sang:

The world's order is in the stars.
We are its children, its orphans.
Cicadas shrill in the willows.

It is not fault, it is not guilt
that has brought us to this. It is
disorder. We were not born to it.

The autumn moon is round and red.
I have not troubled the order,
yet I am no longer in it.

In the first waywardness we could
have gone back. In the second we
began to confuse lost and found.

Had we been angry to be lost,
would we have taken disorder
for order, if any had cared?

Cicadas shrill in the willows.
There was a time we had neighbors.
The autumn moon is round and red.

Men without character took us
into the marshes, neither land
nor river, where we cannot build.

Order is harmony. It is
innovation in tradition.
The autumn moon is round and red.

Elastic words beguiled our ears.
What is the courage worth of fools?
Cicadas shrill in the willows.

Fat faces and slick tongues sold
us disorder for real estate.
The autumn moon is round and red.

The young lord's trees are tender green.
Saplings grow to be useful wood.
Hollow words are the wind blowing.

Cicadas shrill in the willows.
There was a time we had neighbors.
The autumn moon is round and red.

## 10

The dove is over water in Scripture: over the flood with an olive twig in its beak, the rainbow above; over the Jordan with Jesus and John in it, upon the sea as Jonah (which name signifieth *dove*), up out of the sea as Aphrodite (whose totem animal it was). It was the family name of the Admiral of the Ocean Sea.

The horse is the body, its stamina, health, and skills. The hound is faith and loyalty. But symbols are not sense but signs.

Mencius's Chinese cock (tail the color of persimmons, breast the color of the beech in autumn, legs blue) and unimaginable Chinese dog have become under Concord skies a biblical dove, a Rover, and a bay horse. The one is a pet, one is a friend, one is a fellow worker.

We lose not our innocence or our youth or opportunity but our nature itself, atom by atom, helplessly, unless we are kept in possession of it by the spirit of a culture passed down the generations as tradition, the great hearsay of the past.

## 11

Thoreau was most himself when he was Diogenes.

12

One ship *speaks* another when they pass on the high seas. There is a naval metaphor in the paragraph (misprinted as *spoken to* in modern ignorance). Thoreau and his brother John had sailed around the world in August of 1839, all on the Concord and Merrimac, and you could see him in his sailboat on the Concord with a crew of boys, or the smiling Mr. Hawthorne, or the prim Mr. Emerson.

CONVERSATION

The mouse, who left abruptly if Thoreau changed from one tune to another on his flute, was a good listener.
—A man who is moral and chaste, Mr. Thoreau said to the mouse, does not pry into the affairs of others, which may be very different from his own, and which he may not understand.
—O yes! said the mouse. But the affairs of others are interesting. You can learn all sorts of things.
—The housekeeping of my soul may seem a madman's to a Presbyterian or a bear.
The mouse twitched his whiskers. Offered a crumb of hoe-cake, he took it, sitting on Mr. Thoreau's sleeve, sniffed it, and began a diligent chewing.
The mouse knew all about the lead pencils and their inedible shavings, the surveyor's chain, the Anakreon in Greek (edible), the journal with pressed leaves between the pages, the fire (dangerous), the spider family in the corner (none of his business), but it was the flute and the cornmeal that bound him to Mr. Thoreau. And the friendliness.

14

The man under the enormous umbrella out in the snow storm is Mr. Thoreau. Inspecting, as he says. Looking for his dove, his hound, his horse.

## 15

Diogenes was an experimental moralist. He found wealth in owning nothing. He found freedom in being a servant. He discovered that owning was being owned. He discovered that frankness was sharper than a sword. If we act by design, by principle, we need designers. Designers need to search. Mr. Thoreau discovered that the dove is fiercer than a lion when he sat in the Concord jail, like Diogenes. Why should a government come to him to finance its war in Mexico and pay a clergy he could not listen to? Let them find their own money. Let them write laws an honest man can obey. He would write his sentences. That was his genius. Others might find them as useful as he found Diogenes's. The world is far from being over. When Mr. Emerson came to the jail and said, *Henry, what are you doing in here?* and he replied, *Rafe, what are you doing out there?* the words slipped loose like a dove into the spring sky, and were remembered in a London jail by Emmeline Pankhurst, in a South African jail by Mohandas Gandhi, in a Birmingha n jail by Martin Luther King, and cannot be forgotten.

### MEADOW

I remember years ago breaking through a thick oak wood east of the Great Fields and descending into a long, narrow, and winding blueberry swamp which I did not know existed there. A deep, withdrawn meadow sunk low amid the forest, filled with green waving sedge three feet high, and low andromeda, and hardhack, for the most part dry to the feet then, though with a bottom of unfathomed mud, not penetrable except in midsummer or midwinter, and with no print of man or beast in it that I could detect. Over this meadow the marsh-hawk circled undisturbed, and she probably had her nest in it, for flying over the wood she had long since easily discovered it. It was dotted with islands of blueberry bushes and surrounded by a dense hedge of them, mingled with the pannicled andromeda, high chokeberry, wild holly with its beautiful crimson berries, and so on, these being the front rank to a higher wood. Great blueberries, as big as old-fashioned bullets, alternated, or were closely intermingled, with the crimson hollyberries and black chokeberries, in singular contrast yet harmony, and you hardly knew why you selected those only to eat, leaving the others to the birds.

17

This text has been written first with a lead pencil (graphite encased in an hexagonal cedar cylinder) invented by Henry David Thoreau. He also invented a way of sounding ponds, a philosophy for being oneself, and raisin bread.

W. E. B. DUBOIS

Lions have no historians.

WITTGENSTEIN

If a lion could talk, we could not understand him.

20

Fear not, thou drummer of the night, we shall be there.

# Meleager

As a little boy will, for no reason known, stand on one leg
while swinging the other around and back until his pert behind
and heel are in the same cubic foot of space, reaching one arm
down, the other up, so Mikkel Andersen, no longer little, took
this stance, looking out of the top of his eyes, gaping his mouth,
and coming within a hair of losing his balance and that grace
for which fifteen-year-olds seem alone to live.

Sven, his friend and companion for the afternoon, had
come to a military halt as soon as they were in Mikkel's room,
raised an arm straight out, and prodded Mikkel's shoulder with
two fingers.

Mikkel's eyebrows (umber bronze) lifted a quarter inch.

Sven's (silver white) scrunched in.

Mikkel did the little boy on one leg. Upright again, he
searched Sven's laughing eyes.

Each took one step back.

Mikkel's thick hair tumbled onto and hid his forehead. It
spun in a whorl at the top of his head to bunch in feathers over
his ears. His eyes were blue in sunlight, grey green in shadow.
He wore a soccer jersey (collar white) banded with horizontal
mustard and putty green stripes, jeans, stout white socks, and
canvas-topped gym shoes.

In any triangle ABC, all the three angles taken together
are equal to two right angles. To prove this, you must produce
BC, one of its legs, to any distance, suppose to D; then the
external angle ACD is equal to the sum of the two internal
opposite ones CAB and ABC; to both add the angle ACB, then
the sum of the angles ACD and ACB will be equal to the sum

of the angles CAB and CBA and ACB. But the sum of the angles ACD and ACB is equal to two right ones, therefore the sum of the three angles CAB and CBA and ACB is equal to two right angles; that is, the sum of the three angles of any triangle ACB is equal to two right angles.

Sven's hair was cropped close, as he had become impatient with it out orienteering. With the help of Mikkel and solicitude and finally laughter of their scoutmaster he had scissored it down to stubble. A spray of freckles rode from cheek to cheek across his nose.

He wore a loose sweat shirt (dove grey) that hung on his shoulders like the blouses of the horsemen on the Parthenon frieze, and frayed denim short pants (once blue, faded to the color of wood ash by the fanatic regularity of his mother's washdays). Barefoot.

Do what I do, his signing hands said. Mikkel nodded that he understood.

When one line falls perpendicularly on another, as AB on CD, then the angles are right; and describing a circle on the center B, since the angles ABC ABD are equal, their measures must be so too, *id est*, the arcs AC AD must be equal; but the whole CAD is a semicircle, since CD, a line passing through the center B, is a diameter; therefore each of the parts AC AD is a quadrant, *id est* 90 degrees; so the measure of a right angle is always 90 degrees.

Sven gave a nanosecond's glance toward his bare feet. Mikkel sank to one knee and untied the laces of his right shoe. Other knee, left shoe. Placing his shoes neatly side by side, he drew off his socks, folded them square, and put them at the midpoint between himself and Sven, who (from a biography of Kierkegaard) thought of the black tumble of carriage wheels, the nobility of horses, the friendship of dogs, and the meanness of candlelight. Mikkel, knowing that he was to duplicate Sven's imagination, thought of the yellow meadows of Mongolia strewn with blue rocks like huddled saurians.

Sven pulled his shirt over his head. High definition of pectorals, teats wide apart. Fine down in the mesial groove from thorax to navel. Skin Mohican copper. Mikkel copycatted. Torso the twin of Sven's except for ruddier teats and a damp wisp of axial hair in the deltoid furrows.

A figure bounded by four sides is called a quadrilateral or quadrangular figure, as ABDC. Quadrilateral figures whose opposite sides are parallel are called parallelograms. Thus in the quadrilateral figure ABDC, if the side AC be parallel to BD which is opposite to it, and AB be parallel to CD, then the figure ABDC is a parallelogram. A parallelogram having all its sides equal and its angles right is a square.

Sven imagined Erika naked and glossy on the textileless beach, the fuzz, so much darker than her hair, on her plump sex with its covert furrow. Mikkel received this as Professor Pedersen's trendy admonitions, which Erika took off at the polser wagon as *Political! Political!* clucked the hen, *political correctness!* And *Deconstruction!* cawed the crow.

Sven cupped his hand over his crotch. Mikkel, looking merry, shoved his hand deep between his legs, pulling it up in a slow scoop.

Red poultry with blue legs at Grandpa Ib's, whose farmhouse had elvishly small rooms, stairs as steep as a ladder, stone floor in the kitchen, flowers all around the house so that you looked out the windows through hollyhocks and larkspur, the old thrown-glass panes putting spirals and cunning warps into the stable's thatch (with gold and green moss), the meadow with cows and one horse, the dirt road to the village hedged high with hawthorn. He and Mikkel had spent weeks there, sleeping in the narrow feather bed in the attic, rolled into each other by the pliant depth of the mattress.

Mikkel, looking hard into Sven's eyes (while a dog barked down the street and an automobile crunched along the gravel of a drive and killed its motor), decided to confuse the hell out of Sven by stacking images: having a wienerbrød and coffee with Erika in the Arcade (speaking French with, as Erika said, a Swedish accent), Biff in the comicbook the fly of whose jeans bows out in a saddle stain colored yellow, Pastor Tvemunding explaining, with a twinkle in his eye, how Danish liberalism is consonant with the deepest spirit of the church, and how love is always an expression of God's will.

If to any point in a circumference, *videlicet* B, there be drawn a diameter FCB, and from the point B, perpendicular to that diameter, there be drawn the line BH; that line is called a *tangent* to the circle in the point B; which tangent can touch the circle only in one point B, else if it touched it in more, it would go within it, and not be a tangent but a chord.

The tangent of any arc AB is a right line drawn perpendicular to a diameter through the one end of the arc B, and terminated by a line CAH, drawn from the center through the other end A; thus BH is the tangent of the arc AB.

Sven (with satiric modesty) slid his zipper open, pushed his pants down and off. Underpants a minislip from Illum's, size *lille*, dingy white with an ochre smutch on the pouch. Mikkel shoved down his jeans and with some shuffling and plucking got them off. Minislip Dim (*fabriqué en France*), Greek blue with a white waistband.

What an arc wants of a quadrant is called the *complement* of that arc; thus AE, being what the arc AB wants of the quadrant EB, is called the complement of the arc AB. And what an arc wants of a semicircle is called the *supplement* of that arc; thus since AF is what the arc AB wants of the semicircle BAF, it is the supplement of the arc AB.

The sine, tangent, *et caetera*, of the complement of any arc is called the cosine, cotangent, *et caetera* of that arc.

Sven slid his eyes to the right toward the sound of an automobile stopping. Mikkel raised his shoulders a smidgen and showed his palms, either in brave nonchalance or acceptance of the contrariness of fate. They listened for footsteps which they did not hear. Their scoutmaster Stefan Ulfson (from the Fyn, a student in geology) was discussing personal space. Too close, too far. He had asked Mikkel and Sven to stand three meters from each other and start a conversation. You feel awkward at that distance, don't you? Take one step forward and try again. Show us at what distance you feel comfortable and relaxed talking to each other. It was unkind to big Stefan, but they closed the distance between them until they were toe to toe, nose to nose. It was a rabbity scrunch in Sven's nose that made Mikkel certain of the image, and he jounced the neb of his nose in confirmation.

The sine of the supplement of an arc is the same with the sine of the arc itself; for, drawing them according to the definitions, there results the selfsame line. A right-lined angle is measured by an arc of a circle described upon the angular point as a center, comprehended between the two legs that form the angle; thus the angle ABD is measured by the arc AD of the circle CADE that is described upon the point B as a center; and the angle is said to be of as many degrees as the arc is; so if the arc AD be 45 degrees, then the angle ABD is said to be an angle of 45 degrees. Hence the angles are greater or less, according as the arc described about the angular point and terminated by the two legs contains a greater or less number of degrees.

The silence between them was fused with the low-angled late afternoon sunlight that gilded their bodies. Their minds were mirrors of each other. Whether they stood for a minute or half an hour breathing evenly, looking into each other's eyes, before Sven lowered his gaze to Mikkel's briefs and bent forward to remove his own, and Mikkel his, neither could say. Sven's penis jutted limber and rising from a clump of ginger hair that tangled down around his plump scrotum. A disc of glans, with eyelet, filled the foreskin's opening. Mikkel's lifted erect, slipping its foreskin as it rose and grew. His pubic hair was reddish and thicker than Sven's.

From Sven, a simple smile, and sigh, his first sound since they'd come into the room. He tossed his briefs to Mikkel, who drew them on as best he could, considering. Sven waited until he was as erect as Mikkel before pulling on Mikkel's underpants.

The *bil* rolling into the drive was the one they had been listening for. They stepped closer and grinned into each other's eyes. They were dressed when there were sounds of Mikkel's mother and grocery bags in the kitchen.

There is no force however great can stretch a thread however fine into a horizontal line that is absolutely straight.

# Mr. Churchyard and the Troll

When the chessboard in the coffeehouse seemed an idle ruse
to beguile away the hours, and the battlements around Kastel-
let with their hawthorn and green-shanked moorhens and
pacing soldiers ran thin on charm, and his writing balked at
being written, and books tasted stale, and his thoughts became
a snarl rather than a woven flow, Mr. Churchyard, the philosopher, hired a carriage to the Troll Wood for a long speculative
walk.

The lout on the box was eating peasecods from his hat.
—To the Troll Wood, Mr. Churchyard said, tightening the fit
of his gloves.

The sky was Baltic, with North German clouds.

Copenhagen was a thunder of rolling barrels, squeaking
cart wheels, hooting packetboats, Lutheran brass bands, fish
hawkers, a racket of bells.

And impudent imps of boys crying after him *Either! Or!*
while their sisters warned *'E'll turn and gitcha!*

If it were a lucky afternoon, the troll would be in the
wood. Mr. Churchyard knew that this troll, so strangely beautiful in a mushroomy sort of way, was a figment entirely in his
mind, the creature of overwork, indigestion, or bile, perhaps
even original sin, still it was a troll.

Socrates, that honest man, had his daimon, why not Mr.
Churchyard his troll? Its eyes looked at him from among leaves,
above. Its hair was Danish, like thistledown, and was neatly
cut and finished, the shape of a porridge bowl. He did not come
when called. You had to sit on a log, and wait.

The wood was of mountain ash and beech which had

grown thick and dark among flocks of boulders silver with lichen and green with moss. Underfoot, spongy and deep, lay a century's mulch of fallen leaves, through which the odd wild-flower pushed, convolute and colorless of blossom, from the morning of time. We are welcome in meadows, where the carpet is laid down, with grass to eat, if we are cows or field mice, and the yellows and blues are those of the Greek poets and Italian painters.

But here, in the wood, we intrude. Across the sound, in Sweden, there are forests with tall cone-bearing trees, and wolves. Nature has her orders. A wood is as different from a forest as a meadow from a marsh. Owls and trolls live here. And philosophers.

In Plato's grove you heard the snick of shears all morning long, and rakes combing gravel. Epicurus spoke of necessity and fate while watching his grass lawn being rolled smooth. Aristotle and Theophrastus picked flowers in Mytilenian meadows, under parasols. And there was the Swede Linnaeus, as he called himself, who studied nature in Dutch gardens, yawned at by fat English cats.

The troll was somewhere over there, where the leaves shifted.

If Nikolai Grundtvig were here, or Mr. Churchyard's brother, Peter, the bishop, they would invite the troll to join them in a jolly folk dance.

Was that a foot in the ferns, with cunning toes? If there was one troll, there were two. It would have a wife. Nature would have it so. And young. Why should one doubt trolls when the god has kept himself hidden all this time?

When Amos talked with the god, was Amos talking to himself? For the god is hidden in light, in full view, and we cannot see him.

Curled, small fingers in the beech leaves. Fate must drop like a ripe apple. He was not especially eager to see the troll. He was not, despairingly, eager to see the god, even if he could. He had, twice now, seen the troll. It was its singularity that was important. Beyond that he could not think. There was the pure goodness of the god, all but unimaginable, and there was the pure sensuality of Don Giovanni, imaginable with the co-operation of the flesh, and there was the pure intellect of Socrates, easily imaginable, as the mind, that trollish ganglion, like Don Giovanni's mutinous testicles, was a gift from the god.

Hegel's brain in a jar of formaldehyde on the moon.

The troll was another purity, that much was certain, but of what? Your coachman, Mr. Churchyard, is sitting out there, beyond the copse, picking his nose and waiting.

The troll had said its name was Hitch. Was it of an order, upward from the mushroom (which, he could now see, it was munching) as angels are an order downward from the god? He did not see it as one finds Napoleon in the drawing of two trees, where you find his figure delineated by the branches, but as an image soaking through the fabric of vision, leaf-and-berry eyes, peanut toes, sapling legs. An acorn for sex.

—There are interstices, Mr. Churchyard said, taking off his tall hat and setting it on the log, through which things fall. In one of the spurious gospels, for instance, there is Jesus choosing Simon from among the fishers drawing up their net. And with Jesus is his dog. Or a dog.

—Yes, Lord, Simon says, coming willingly.

—And when he calls you again, says the dog, you are to answer to the name Peter.

This has been edited out of the gospels as we have them, by some high-minded copyist who did not notice that an animal whose whole soul is composed of loyalty and whose faith in his master cannot be shaken by any force, neither by death nor by distance, is given a voice, like Balaam's ass centuries before, to remind us that our perception of the otherworldly is blind.

And then in a fanciful *Acts of the Apostles* there's a talking lion who works as a pitch for Paul and Barnabas.

—Hello folks! Though I am only a numble beast, and have no theology, I'm here to get your attention and invite you to rally around and listen to my dear friends C. Paulus, a Roman citizen, and Joseph Consolation Barnabas, who have a message for you.

A blue-eyed lion, washed and fluffed for his public appearance, paws as big as plates.

Was that the troll, there, peeping from behind a tree? —We met last autumn, Mr. Churchyard said in a voice he used for children, when the sky was packed with clouds like hills of dirty wool, and a mist smoked along the ground. You would not, you know, tell me your name, and so I named you Hitch, by your leave, taking silence for assent. How have you fared since then?

There was a flicker of leaves, a deepening of the wood's silence.
—You are not afraid, are you, of my walking stick leaning here against the log? It is just a length of wood with a silver knob which gentlemen in Copenhagen carry about with them. It goes with my hat here, and my gloves. They make a set of things to indicate to the world that we have money and that we pretend to morals approved of by the police and the clergy. Come out into the open.

In a shared fish, said Demokritos, there are no bones.
—So let me tell you a story that may shed light on our predicament. There was once a highwayman in England who disguised himself with a great bagwig, such as the noted Samuel Johnson was the last to wear in polite society. When a wayfarer came along the road he worked, so to speak, he emerged from behind a bush, giving the wayfarer the choice of giving up his money or his life. The frightened wayfarer quailed at his pistol, and probably at his wig, and turned over to him his horse and purse.

The highwayman, riding away, threw the wig by the side of the road, where a pedestrian later found it, and put it on as windfall finery.

Meanwhile, the wayfarer who had been robbed came to a town where the pedestrian with his newfound wig had also just arrived. The wayfarer, seeing him, called out for the bailiff and had him charged before the magistrate with highway robbery. He would, he testified, know that wig anywhere.

The magistrate sentenced the pedestrian to be hanged.

Now this was a small town, and the assizes drew a large crowd, among whom was the highwayman.

—Fool! he cried out to the magistrate. You are sending an innocent man to the gallows. Look, give me the wig, and I will put it on and say, *Your money or your life*, and this false accuser will see his mistake. *Yes, yes!* the accuser said. That is the voice I heard from under the great wig.

The magistrate, however, ruled that the first identification was made under oath, before God, and that the sentence, pronounced through the majesty of the law, had been passed. And must stand.

Surely there was a shifting of shadows over there, between the Norway pine and the larch, upward and sideways, where the troll must be.

It would be charming if the troll looked like a Danish child, if it upended itself and stood on its head, pedalling its feet in the air and turning pink in the face. Or stand on its right leg with its left foot hooked around its neck, like the Gypsy acrobats on market day.

—The law, you see, is unbending. We made the law after the manner of the god, so it has nothing human in it. Let me tell you about the god. When he brought his people out of bondage in Aegypt, he led them to Kanaan, but for forty years they wandered in the desert, where the god fed them with a white fluffy bread, manna it was called, of which they became tired. So they asked for something different, something savory. Like quails, quails roasted brown on a spit over a fire, basted in their own juice, salted and rubbed with sage. So the god, who was in a proper snit about their ingratitude and greed, with their placing the sensuality of taste before a just appreciation of his grandeur and might, said:

—Ye shall eat until it comes out of your nose!

And a hail of dead quail fell from the sky, and his people

dressed and cooked them, and (here I quote Scripture) even as the meat was yet in their teeth, the god caused a deadly plague to kill them who had eaten of the quail.

—What do you think of that? It was a prayer he was answering.

The troll's eyes were those of a happy child and therefore unreadable, for a child's happiness is something we have all had to forget. It is a happiness that comes from wrenching the hands off the clock, of pitching Grandpa's false teeth in the fire, of stealing, of lying, of pulling the cat's tail, of shattering the china vase, of hiding from one's parents to make them sick with worry, of hitting one's best friend's toes with the hammer. Of a child with beautiful hair, as if of spun and curled gold, and with big blue eyes, culture says *behold an angel!* and nature says *here is your own personal devil.*

A bird in those branches, or the troll?

—Listen! he said. You see me here in my great coat of German cut (in which I have heard Schelling lecture, for German auditoria are as cold as Greenland), gloves, stovepipe trews, cane, and handkerchief up my sleeve, but you cannot see from any of this, from my large nose or the fact that my brother Peter is a bishop, that I live in a city of merchants who imagine themselves to be Christians. You might as well say that a banjo player from Louisiana is Mozart.

You cannot guess from any of this that my father once shook his fist at the god on a hill in Jylland, and cursed him to his face.

The troll, the troll! But no: a hare or fox whose home this wood is.

Trolls belonged, Mr. Churchyard imagined, to the genera of toadstools, in the same way that trees were kin to angels. Mr. Churchyard's century was looking into nature, and the Germans were scrutinizing Scripture. Why have the god, after all, when they have Hegel?

Were not there passages in Scripture where the scribes wrote the opposite of what mercy and fear suggested that they suppress? Abraham most certainly sacrificed Isaac.

His father had cursed the god and moved to Copenhagen and prospered as a merchant, money begetting money in his coffers. He died in the arms of angels bearing him to heaven.

The corollary, is it not, is that if we pray we are answered with death while the meat of the quail is yet in our teeth. But the world is here, and to despair is sin. Even in their churches the tall light, the ungiving hard January light in the high windows bespeaks that worldliness of the world which no Hegelianism can pretend isn't there, isn't here.

Mr. Churchyard lifted his specs onto his forehead, ran his little finger along an eyebrow, massaged his nose, closed his eyes, licked the corners of his mouth, and coughed softly.

The irony of it.

A horse was as alive as he, and a cow had exactly as much being. A midge.

It would be some comfort if he could know that he was precisely as ugly as Socrates. He was, like all Danes, beautiful in his youth. Then his nose had grown and grown, and his back had warped, and his digestion gone to hell.

Perhaps the troll was not the size he thought it was, and was wrapped in a leaf.

Whatever we say of the god that he isn't, he is.

—*Absconditus* we say he is, seeing him everywhere. What's with us, O Troll, that we have faith in the unseen, unheard, and untouched, while rejecting what's before our eyes? In the mists of despair I see that we prefer what isn't to what is. We place our enthusiasm in scriptures we don't read, or read with fanciful misunderstanding, taking our unknowing for knowing. Our religion's a gaudy superstition and unlicensed magic.

Mr. Churchyard knew that the troll was behind one of the trees before him. He felt it as a certainty. He would have, when seen, a flat nose, round green eyes, a frog's mouth, and large ears.

—Listen! This Sunday past, in the palace church, the court chaplain, who is very popular and who in his bishop's robes looks like a Byzantine emperor, preached a sermon to a select congregation of fat merchants, lawyers, bankers, and virgins. He preached with eloquence and resonating solemnity. His text was *Christ chose the lowly and despised.* Nobody laughed.

The afternoon was getting on and the sky was graying over with clouds. Mr. Churchyard decided to make a bargain with himself, a leap of faith. He would believe the troll was there, and not bother whether it was or not. An event is real insofar as we have the desire to believe it. Bishop Mynster preached his eloquent sermon because Mr. Churchyard's father had admired him, not because Mr. Churchyard was sitting between an outlaw dressed as a merchant banker and a lady whose bonnet was made in London. He heard Bishop Mynster for his father's sake. He would converse with the troll for his own sake.

And so, the troll. He was not prepared for it to be naked. Its Danish, when it spoke, was old.

An urchin from up around Swan's Mill. It put out an arm for balance, standing on one leg, swinging the other back and forth.

—Be you a frog? it asked.

—I am a human being.

—Could have fooled me. What way comest ye, through or under?

It was amused by the consternation on Mr. Churchyard's face and crimped the corners of its mouth.

—If through color, that be the one way, to butt through yellow into blue, through red to green. T'other way's to back up a little, find a place to get through, and wiggle in. Through the curve, at the tide. Even's one, odd the other.

The troll came closer. Mr. Churchyard could see a spatter of freckles on its cheeks and nose. It cautiously touched his walking stick.

—Ash, it said. I did not know the tree. Always on this side, one moon with another, bayn't ye?

—This side of what? Mr. Churchyard asked quietly.

—Ye've never been inside the mullein, have ye? Never in the

horehound, the milkweed, the spurge? What be you?

—I am a Dane. What if I were to ask you what you are? You are to my eye a boy, with all the accessories, well fed and healthy. Are you not cold, wearing nothing?

The troll raised a leg, holding its foot in its hand, so that its shin was parallel to the forest floor. It grinned, with or without irony Mr. Churchyard could not say. Its thin eyebrows went up under its hair.

—Let me say, Mr. Churchyard said, that I am certain you are in my imagination, not there at all, though you smell of sage or borage, and that you are a creature for which our science cannot account. When we think, we bind. I have not yet caught you. I don't even know what or who you are. Now where does that get us?

—But I am, the troll said.

—I believe you. I want to believe you. But this is the nineteenth century. We know everything. There is no order of beings to which you could belong. Do you know the god?

The troll thought, a finger to its cheek.

—Be it a riddle? What have ye for me if I answer right?

—How could it be a riddle if I ask you if you know the god? You do, or you don't.

—Be you looking hereabouts for him?

—I am.

—What be his smell? What trees be his kinfolk?

—I've never seen him. No description of him exists.

—How wouldst ye know did you find him?

—I would know him. There would be a feeling.

—Badger, squirrel, fox, weasel, hopfrog, deer, owl, grebe, goose, one of them? Or pine, oak, elderberry, willow, one of them? Elf, kobold, nisse, one of us? Spider, midge, ant, moth?

The troll then arranged itself, as if it had clothes to tidy the fit of, as if it were a child in front of a class about to recite. It sang. Its voice had something of the bee in it, a recurring hum and buzz, like the *Barockfagott* in Monteverdi's *Orfeo*, and something of the ringdove's hollow treble. The rhythm was a country dance's, a jig. But what were the words?

Mr. Churchyard made out *the horse sick of the moon* and *the owl who had numbers*. The refrain sounded Lappish. *One fish, and another, and a basket of grass.*

When the song was over, Mr. Churchyard bent forward in an appreciative bow. Where had he heard the melody, at some concert of folk music? At the Roskilde market? And had he not seen the troll itself, astoundingly dirty, in patched clothes and blue cap, on the wharf at Nyhavn?

And then there was no troll, only the forest floor and the damp green smell of the wood, and the ticking of his watch.

That the god existed Socrates held to be true with an honest uncertainty and deep feeling. We, too, believe at the same risk, caught in the same contradiction of an uncertain certainty. But now the uncertainty is different, for it is absurd, and to believe with deep feeling in the absurd is faith. Socrates's knowing that he did not know is high humor when compared to something as serious as the absurd, and Socrates's deep feeling for the existential is cool Greek wit when compared to the will to believe.

# O Gadjo Niglo

In the summer they bring the artillery and fire out to sea. The officers in their red coats arrive the day before on glossy horses. The caissons and powder wagons come through the woods at night. In the morning the cannons sit battery by battery on the beach.

The sergeants give the orders for unlimbering and spreading trails. The gunner opens the breech and seats the shell and charge. A lieutenant gives the quadrant and deflection to a corporal who shouts them to the gunners who run the barrels up and wind them to the side with a crank on a wheel. An order to fire at the top of the corporal's lungs and the gunners pull the lanyards. The cannons crack and jump. A line of splashes far out at sea.

I watched all this from my place in the bushes on the hill above. The old officer pulled his moustache. There was a grand haze into which the cannon smoke ran like ink in water. The thrushes and sparrows ripped from the bushes when the cannons boomed. The gulls fluttered and scattered. I was Robinson Crusoe observing from my covert the army of the emperor that had come to practise its aim on the shores of my island.

Once when an officer came to the door I could see close up his sword and shoulder belt. His eyes were grey with lashes like a girl. The colonel would be obliged for the loan of a lemon had we such an article to spare. Thesmond glided away and returned with a lemon on a salver. It was wrapped in a twist of tissue. Thesmond nodded briefly to the charm of his smile.

Why ever a lemon? Matilda would ask such a question. It was her nature. She gave me one of her looks. Thesmond said that it was for the colonel's drink before dinner. To Papa he would have said for the colonel's preprandial impotation. Tie your tongue. So colonels had dinner out there in their tents on the scrub. I had seen the soldiers file past the field kitchens and eat on the rocks out of tin plates. Sometimes they wrestled.

Toward evening they stripped naked and swam in the sea. Some were as white as plaster and some were as brown as an acorn. The officers bathed separately. Orderlies had towels for them when they came panting and knocking water from their ears.

The officer who came to the door on his roan was as hairy as a rug down his front when he undressed for the sea. Thickest just under his throat and across his chest and between his legs. I saw his peter good.

I could still hear the cannon at night along with the dull roar of the sea. Over two hills and a valley. The road to the beach is off our road to the turnpike. The caissons rattle and creak along it back to wherever they come from. Back to Stockholm. Back to Göteborg. In a week the ruts and marks will be smoothed by the wind.

Next day the gypsies go over the place looking and picking up. They come from nowhere like the artillery and go off as suddenly. They will steal me if I let them see me. Matilda can recall the names of boys taken off by the gypsies. Nor must I go near the artillery because of the gunpowder and the talk.

The artillery came this year after Stilt. How could I have escaped Stilt to see them? He comes in the winter and stays for months. He replaced Fröken Gomber who taught me when I was little. Svensk and arithmetic. Geography and history. Stilt teaches me geometry and rhetoric. Latin and compound interest. He himself goes to school when he is not here. He is writing a thesis in divinity which is about matters which he says I could not yet begin to comprehend. Free will and destiny. Election and grace.

Stilt bends and kisses Grandmama's old hand to her merriment though her scrunch of fun is all gone when he stands straight again. He comments on the golden weather. She says that it will change. She asks him to witness the instability of the candle flames and the thickness of the squirrels' coats. There is moreover an early red in the larches.

For Stilt I am ordered into jacket and tie. I must have clean fingernails. He cleans his while we read Latin. He smells of peppermint. Vercingetorix. Helvetia. Cisalpine Gauls.

In the summer there is no Stilt.

Papa comes and goes and stays only a little while. He is very busy. He always brings wonderful things. The microscope which Stilt has taught me to use is the most wonderful though I have liked better my model ship.

Grandmama is in her room. She is little and cold all the time. Every morning we kneel around her and say our prayers. We hear Scripture and we hear Swedenborg. And she gets off the subject. She will say in the middle of scripture that titled coaches used to come to the door. Thesmond brings the big bible and opens it on a table that sits over Grandmama's knees. Thessalonians. Galatians. We hear that all of heaven is one angel just as all of mankind is one man except that he fell away from grace.

With Stilt I look at leaves under the microscope. I draw a stoma. An arrangement of cells at the stem and at the edge of the leaf.

Papa looks like Sir Charles Wheatstone in the stereopticon.

In the summer with no Stilt I found it easy to sneak away to the stables to find Tarpy the miller's son. He is not the miller's son but the miller's bastard. The miller flies into a rage if you tease him about whose son he is. I have heard that he is the bastard of the miller's wife got on her by a drummer who sells needles and thread. Old Sollander raised him on our place. He would say tried to raise him.

Sometimes when I find him he has his usual crazy sweetness in his eyes and tears too which he wipes with his rotten sleeves. Sollander has crisscrossed welts up his legs. Some on his arms. And one across his forehead beading blood. He is older than I but a baby. The predikant says that we are not to associate with him. He is vile and depraved. I learned that for myself down by the river collecting beetles. He was there smiling as wide as the urchins in the funny German picture books. He was wearing my cast off breeches mended beyond mending more and a jacket that had been Papa's. His hair was cut any which a way and combed with fingers if combed at all. His smile bloomed into huggermugger. He asked to see my peter and showed me his. I felt lucky and liked his friendliness and his interest.

I think I knew that his welts were something to do with his peter and his playing with it lots. I knew that the predikant had given Sollander leave to beat this vileness out of Tarpy. So I balked. And knew that my stubbornness was a false face.

I lied and said that I didn't do such things. All the while there was to my mind a rammy prestige that went with his goatishness. Of a man who butts down doors with his head you can only say that he butts down doors with his head. But he is not a niddering about it and does it with a will. Tarpy had his peter out of his fly. It was bigger and longer than mine.

In times of temptation you must think of the angels. Their wide ears are always before your mouth. They move beside you tread for tread. No man is ever utterly alone. They are in trees. They love a thicket and a still place. Yet Grandmama says they have houses of their own for all their sitting in nooks of ours and cities of their own.

She has seen her grandfather the sea captain against the ceiling of the library as if he were floating upward and could get no farther. She says I must look for the angels in my rambles. She says that with my innocent eyes I should be able to see the most distinguished spirits. Gold or silver they will seem to my eyes. I am to remember that in seeing one angel I am seeing all of heaven.

The angels are clothed in a vesture of light. The best are

dressed in clinging fire. All is by degree with Swedenborg and
the angels inmost to God are naked and are the beautifullest of
all. I think I have seen what Grandmama and old Emmanuel
mean by angel. You go by signs. The sign of an angel is *influx*.
One of her words. One of his words. There is an influx of angel
body into a hedge of wild roses when the light is level at morning and when it is downward at noon and level again toward
evening. There are tall angels in the larches. Round angels in
sunflowers.

*Stirk* everybody said he was. I could not tell luck from
pitfall. I followed him down the thistle path to the willows by
the river. He went to a sand bank where the bears fish in winter. He pushed his breeches down. I played at chucking rocks
and poking around the place as if it were new to me. I gave
several interested glances and said I had to be going. He looked
hurt and had just been thrashed. That we were not friends did
not help my feelings as I walked away. If he was a halfwit I
was a liar. Two kinds of shame tussled in me. But I kept climbing the path. Stubbornness is always a kind of treason.

I could not look into the microscope without thinking of
him. He was in the stereopticon. He haunted me under the
covers. Everywhere. Let the air be as thick with angels as snow
I would still be jealous of his doings. Better a halfwit than a
prig. I caught glimpses of him along the river or on the knolls.
He was always alone.

I made myself a promise. I would not walk away the next
time. The promise itself was a pleasure.

The pounce came one afternoon when I saw Tarpy squat-
ting in the river sand drawing with a stick. All I saw from
above was the mess of hair. Strudel as it was you could see the
verticillus commanding the whorl. I chucked a rock over his
head to splash just beyond him. He looked miserable and
lonely. He jumped at the splash and I hollered cheerfully to
reassure him. His eyes were suspicious. I looked at his drawing.
An eddy of lines like water or hair.

He asked me right off if I wanted to see a fox's den. I

squatted beside him to add closeness to my bravery. Did he feel like playing with his peter? I whispered. He grinned.

I led this time and in a roundabout way that was meant to be casual brought us to our barn from the back where a ladder goes up to the loft. We looked at the tracks of a hare on the way. He said it was a buck in its first year. He showed me deer droppings. An owl's nest.

The loft was dim and cozy. I was sorry to be so clean when he was shoddy and dirty. I shamelessly took my breeches off and made myself comfortable on a heap of feed sacks. My forehead and the back of my neck tingled because I'd not done it with anybody watching. Only in bed or in the copse or back of the stables. Or secretly in my breeches. Tarpy used a slower pull and tigged his chin with his tongue.

I'd seen Pelser the blacksmith's boy jiggling away at his lizard's tail of a peter and Nock the stablehand swanking his stang from pucker to stark but the one was being silly and the other larking on a dare. Here was Tarpy with his big peter in his neaf all rumpled with knobs and veins and the mull of its nozzle fat as a table plum with a slanting warp from the thirl of the tuck to the belling out of the rim. It made my mouth dry to watch him thwack it full stretch.

He had less hair than I above his peter. His was ginger. Mine was springy and black. He asked if mine felt good. He slid his foot out and waggled it against mine. We were friends. He said we could make it last or come quick and then come again. I was near enough to my sneeze to say quick. My milky drop jumped out. Tarpy took longer to reach his sneeze and a hot blush spread up my back and slid down again as a chill when I saw the amount of spunk that he spurted. A blob spattered two feet away. Another fell just short of the first. A third ran into his fingers.

We did it again later in the afternoon on the sand bank where the bears fish in winter. He let me feel his peter. He asked me if I could get him a piece of pie. I told him to meet me just before sunset between the knoll and the river. I brought him the drumstick of a hen and a fair slab of gooseberry pie. I had never seen anyone eat so. He cleaned the bone with his teeth and broke it and sucked out the marrow.

He could not read. I told him *Robinson Crusoe*. He said he knew the ABCs but had the order all crazy when he tried to say them. He made some of the letters backward in the sand where we wrote them out.

We met every day. I would see Tarpy in the sunflowers from my window and put down my Fenimore Cooper or Baron von Humboldt and go out with my beetle bottle and kit. Matilda would cry that I needed a straw hat against sun stroke. I would head for the woods on the bluff over the sea. Tarpy would bob up to my left when we were out of sight of the house. In a glacial scoop ringed with a haw of bushes under a boulder we shed our breeches and fell to. I liked to loll awhile before the delicious business and pry into Tarpy's abandon with curiosity and envy. He would have come several times since we'd jacked off the day before.

He lay back in the grass with one hand under his head and the other on his peter like a big stemmed pink mushroom. It is as I've measured fourteen centimetres long. And there is a mushroom like Tarpy's peter. *Phallus impudicus*. Mine is twelve but growing. The more you play with it the bigger it gets. Three times and we would go on a ramble for beetles. One more time standing in the wheatfield dangerously near the house before I was expected to be in.

Morning and afternoon we zinged our spunk in the woods along the river and above the sea. I got bolder and sneaked out after dark to meet Tarpy in the barn loft. Sometimes he did me and I him.

We met Old Sollander on the road. He started right in. No good would come of our playing together. He tapped his open hand with his stick. What if he told the squire what we did? Tarpy pulled my shirt so that I would be with him when he ran. I said that I could be friends with who I wanted.

He showed me a long flat rock way back in a part of the

woods where I had never been. It had pictures chiselled into it. He showed me how to see the reindeer. We cleared some moss and lichen away and found a dragon boat. The mast. The oars. Vikings in it rowing. And there was a Viking with his peter up.

One day I turned up at the river with a bundle and said he would see when he asked what I had. Breechesless we got snug shoulder to shoulder in a bush and jacked a sweetness into our peters. We took our time. We were learning to make it last for a lovely long time. The sunshine was scattered in the trees and made the river blue in its middle.

The crickets sang as loud as a waterfall. Swarms of midges hung out over the water. He let me feel the knobby stalk of his peter and jack it for awhile. After we shot off I asked him to do me a favor and ask no questions until I was through with what I was going to do. I unwrapped my bundle. First scissors and comb. He sat crosslegged and naked while I cut his hair. I combed out the rat's nests and elf locks. I knew how to get a strand in the comb and clip it even with the scissors. How to keep combing it down until I had it all of a length across the neck and forehead. I trimmed allowances for the ears.

Then the shampoo. We stood in the river up to our butts. There were welts across his back from beatings that must have cut to the ribs. I lathered up his hair and dug around in it with my fingers. He rinsed it with a duck. I lathered it again. We kept it up until no more black clouded into the water when he ducked. Then the soap. I stood him on a rock and had him all suds. I even brought a wash rag. He jibed only at the hard work in the ears. He squealed when I washed his peter and behind as clean as the river itself. His knees and elbows took some doing. I trimmed his nails and reamed the gunk out from under them with a green twig.

His hair was drying a different color by the time we'd lain on the rock and dried good. I showed him the rest of the bundle. He put the clean shirt on and did a prance like a dandy. Then breeches that might split in the crotch before the day was out. We looked like brothers. We threw his rotten clothes in the river. I told him his new name. Sven.

But he wouldn't have a new name. He would go to the big house with me and walk boldly in past Thesmond and Matilda and act like a friend I had met but he would not have a new name. I argued that if I told them he was Tarpy they would shoo him out. I would go too. He would get me chased out of my own house. He said that they would know he was Tarpy.

I would teach him botany and algebra. I would write Papa and tell him that Tarpy the miller's bastard is not an idiot as people say. That I have given him a bath and some of my clothes and am teaching him subjects. After I teach him to read and write. That he is really clever and deserves better than to live with Old Sollander who is an ignorant man and beats him without cause.

My room is at the top of the house with a window in a gable that looks out into the same larches that Grandmama can see from her window and a window that looks over the sward where the drive comes up. I have a map of the world in colors. A picture of Alexander von Humboldt in the Amazon jungle with his friend Bonpland and an Indian. A cabinet of beetles and moths. A long table with a microscope. Fossils. Books.

My fireplace has a brass bonnet and a fender.

This is where I brought Tarpy the day I washed him and dressed him in clean decent clothes. He ran his fingers along the edges of things as if to appreciate the carpentry. He was looking at the rug when I tried to show him the microscope. Then he was interested in the windowpanes. He made on over the turned mahogany handle of the poker. He wondered at the lamp. And he was anxious to leave.

Once we were well into the wood on the way to the bluffs he said that Thesmond's eyes had been on us all the time. Had I not heard him tiptoe upstairs? Had I not seen him behind the door as we left?

Then he said he would be beaten for the clothes I had put on him. And for being clean. Things not talked about go away so I jollied him into going to our place on the bluffs and told him more of *Robinson Crusoe*. I was carefully keeping Friday back until the right moment.

We had found a sloughed snake skin on the way. A tortoise shell. A coughball from an owl which Tarpy saw and I would have missed. A cockchafer. A hawk feather.

There were seals among the islands which we watched for a long while. The woadwaxen was in flower. The whin. His hand slid under me as we lay on the moss looking down onto the inlet and gave me a fine squeeze. I rolled over and unbuttoned. He was better at it than I could be. I studied his face. The blue of his eyes was speckled gold. I poked a dimple to see the smile. I told him that I thought the world of him and would give him as stout a pleasure as I could once I had shivered and shot off. Don't I know it? he said.

When I got back toward suppertime Matilda hailed me in. I had a green snake and she kept her distance. She had a letter from Papa in which he said he was sending up a person who was to help around the grounds and who was to be a kind of companion to me for the summer. It was a university student who wanted a rural place for the vacations. What did I think of that? She pushed her glasses up onto her hair. I didn't like it.

When was he coming? The letter didn't say. But soon. Matilda said she couldn't think what Papa meant by help around the grounds. He was to have the room above the stables. That was hopeful. I could not imagine Stilt in the room above the stables.

I told Tarpy and Tarpy opened his eyes round and wide and whistled. I said that I could always get away. Mayhap this intruder took naps like Stilt. I explained to Tarpy that people from far away wrote letters and read books. He was not to worry.

When a rainy day kept us apart I looked out the windows and fidgeted. Cook chased me out of the kitchen for inspecting the potato bin and talking about poison. I curled up in a window seat with Canot's *Natural Philosophy*. I looked at the pic-

tures of Pompeii in the big French book. In the stereopticon I
looked at the Suez Canal. The Tour Eiffel. The Hague. Steam-
boats on the Mississippi. Indian sachems who looked like
Lapps.

If I made a dash from the carriage porch to the great oak
to the well I would be close enough to sprint to the barn. It
was the Algonquin Lapp in the stereopticon gave me the idea.
They have second sight. They know things at a distance. Like
old Swedenborg who was part Lapp. I have known before that
Tarpy would be in our place on the knoll and got there so sure
that I unbreeched before I arrived and jumped the brim of the
hollow bare butt. He was there. Waiting. Tarpy was for a certainty in the cozy barn loft watching the rain through the hay
door and waiting for me.

It was dry under the oak though I was wet from the run.
I was wetter when I got to the well house and drenched when I
got to the high dark of the barn where the wet lifted all the
smells to a pitch. The roast smell of oats. The dusty smell of
burlap and the cold smell of graith and shares.

Tarpy grinned down at me from the top of the ladder. I
sneezed going up. We hung my blouse and breeches on nails
and dried me on Tarpy's shirt. I did him first. His fun is transi-
tive and makes me all hot cheeked and dry mouthed so that
my turn goes the better for it. We spurted again with our own
hands.

He had brought me a freckled snail shell which he said I
could have. It was a species I had not seen. Would I show him its
picture in a book? And how did it get there? I told him. He was
getting the grasp of things in their kinship. He liked it that a
cow is a kind of deer and the raccoon a cousin of the bear.

Spiders walked down the air. Birds chittered. Tarpy asked
me if I had brought something to eat and I was ashamed that
I had not thought of it. He knew things to eat in the forest.
Sour berries and roots with the taste of ginger and peppergrass.

There were days when I did not see him at all and I knew
that he was kept in by Old Sollander. There would be new

welts when I saw him again. He never mentioned them. I learned to wait patiently for him in one of our places with meat that I had pocketed at table and pie filched from the kitchen. I sneaked him clean shirts and breeches. The deliciousness I was learning to play into my peter was sweeter and grander by the day.

One afternoon after our ramble I was told that I was to go see Matilda as soon as I got home. Thesmond said so with a singsong in his voice. She had a lace handkerchief crushed in her knuckles when I went to her room. She was sipping tea. For strength. *Jens.* I don't know what we're going to do with you. Your Papa asked me to write him all about your taking up with this wild boy Tarpy. Is that not his name?

I nodded that it was.

She touched the handkerchief to the corner of an eye and said in a sagging voice that she had written Papa as truthfully as she knew how. There are some things which a woman cannot say to a man. I said that you had done just that. Taken up with this boy who is not bright. In his reply (she touched her fingers to the envelope on the table) he says that you are to be commended for sharing your clothes with one so unfortunate and for introducing him to hygiene.

Is that all? I asked.

She sighed and gave me one of her looks. She added that I was to expect a parcel in the post. From Papa. She mashed the handkerchief and clearly had something else to say. What it was she kept to herself.

Get what for? Thesmond asked outside.

For what? I replied in my best teasing voice.

He stiffened and raised his eyebrows. He remarked that it is written in Scripture that thy foot shall slip in time. I was to remember that. I was to remember that as you remember stepping barefoot on a rotten pear thick with hornets.

The fine summer morning when the urge was warm and tingly in my peter I felt as randy about my new canvas satchel with its specimen vials which Papa had sent me as the expecta-

tion of meeting Tarpy for a rich long pull. I had a new natural-
ist's journal and a box of colored pencils smelling cedary from
being sharpened before I set out. I was spry and giddy. I even
wore the straw hat without being told to by Matilda. The journal had a canvas envelope all its own with a flap that buckled
down. I would draw every leaf and inflorescence and write its
name and Linnaean binomial beneath.

I was over the knoll and into the spinney when the wonder of the satchel and bottles and journal all rucked in my
ballocks like beady cider and I began looking for Tarpy. I
whistled for him at the river. He was not about.

So I patiently drew an oxalis with its pale yellow pentad
of petals and its cloverish leaves. Wood sorrel. The pencils
shaded well and I'd never drawn better. I wanted a splendid
page that I could show with pride. My hope was that Tarpy
would come through the thicket behind me and double my
pleasure with surprise. Down the knoll. Up the other side of
the river. The sun on his hair. I wanted to see him shining in
his grin and pugging the snoot of his breeches with a frisky
hand.

I moseyed up to the sea bluffs. He was not in the scoop. I
drew the leaf and acorn of a white oak. A woodpecker thucked
in flurries high up. A spink fifed in the service and was answered with a trill from the beech. I gave the *hoot hoot* we
used. And sharpened my ears. There was only the woods rustle
and wash of the sea. The birds. The crazy woodpecker.

I maundered over most of our rambling ground before I
went back for lunch. At first I had been disappointed and this
was selfish I told myself. Then I was put out. Selfish too. Then
wondering. But he would come from nowhere in the afternoon
as was his way.

Except that he didn't. I looked in the barn loft. Even
around Old Sollander's. I kept my ears cocked for the hoot or
the whistle far into the night. I fell asleep in my clothes in a
chair by the window.

Next morning I watched Old Sollander's cabin through

the rush brake. I had a slice of ham still hot in my satchel and a sandwich of gooseberry jam. If Tarpy was ill I ought to go direct to the door and ask. I should have asked yesterday.

Looking for Tarpy? Sollander said from behind me.

I jumped. He studied my face. He seemed to have on too many clothes. Strings tied everywhere. Strings holding his waistcoat together at the buttonholes. Waistcoats. At least two of them. Strings closing the collar of his shirt. Strings tying his cuffs.

Tarpy's gone. You won't see Tarpy anymore.

I heard the words but could not think what they meant.

Aye. To an institution we've sent him. For his own good. Mind you that. For his own good.

Tears blinded my eyes or I would have spoken. Or asked how and when. Or bloodied him with a rock. As it was I could only swing my canvas satchel from my shoulder and with a windup once around my head hit him full in the face with it. But his stick was up. It hit with a whomp.

I ran. I wanted to run anywhere but home but that is where I went. Awful ideas got into my head. It numbed me that perhaps Papa had arranged for it all. I rejected that. The miller did it. Not that either. The miller was as ignorant as Sollander. Did they do it for meanness? Had Tarpy done something I didn't know about?

I ran past Thesmond and to my room. I wouldn't come out when they shouted at me in the hall. I lay across the bed and cried until I saw how selfish that was. For Tarpy's trouble I was doing the crying. Helping nothing and nobody.

First of all I would kill Sollander. Horribly. To pay him for every welt on Tarpy's body. He had earned his death and I was the one to give him payment in full. I had given Tarpy pleasure and warmth and friendliness and he had given him pain. He would have all the pain back. I would do it with an ax. Slowly. So that he could dread the next blow.

Then I would make a speech before everybody so that Papa could understand. And Stilt. And Thesmond and Matilda.

No. That was not the thing to do. I would kill him and say nothing. People would talk for years about the mystery of his death and I would gloat over my secret.

Getting Tarpy out of the institution would be harder than killing Sollander. I would get Tarpy out instead of wasting time butchering Sollander. I would show him. Then we would run off together.

Matilda and Thesmond had got into the room I don't know how. They made me drink spoonsful of something black and bitter. Even Grandmama came.

I dreamed all night of lumber shifting in a room. I was trying to arrange it. It slid away from itself when I stacked it. I stumbled. Sweated. The room was hot. The lumber was rough and splintery. It crashed around me. I moved it piece by piece only to have it tumble back.

They dried me with towels and kept a fire all day in the room. I stared at the window with its curtains half drawn and then I was in the museum Papa took me to and Tarpy was with us. We were all three in a carriage that rolled down the turnpike. It was a frosty morning and we were happy. The happiness turned to dread for no reason that I could understand. We were in North Harbor. We had rugs over our knees.

We stopped for hot milk and honey bread at an inn. Everybody stood around a great fire. The floor was brick like our kitchen. Papa drank an *akvavit* from a little glass with a stem.

Then we were on a schooner. So many tackles slide up and down and the sailors wind the anchor out of the sea. The sails go up and you feel the living shiver as it starts to move.

By night we put in at a city with many ships docked right at a street. We are on a train.

I scream. Matilda is on the train except that it is not a train but my room and she is folding a wet washcloth and pressing it cool against my forehead.

We are in a museum in the city where Papa has taken us. We see a narwhale. Minerals. Cabinets of wax fruit. There is a dragon ship of the Vikings filling a whole room. The reared snake's head of its prow rises above us.

We are very busy in the city. We must buy Grandmama a shawl from Scotland. Matilda has specified many spools of thread that we are to bring back. I am in a sailor suit. Tarpy is in a sailor suit. We sleep in the same deep bed in the hotel in the city. Our peters are as sweet as jam and as tingling as cider when we push them together side by side under the eiderdown.

There is a man with a peg leg selling newspapers in the street. A Negro with a red kerchief for a hat. Horses in slings loaded onto ships. A military band marches past the King's palace. We eat roast chestnuts at a stand.

I have peed the bed. Thesmond washes me in alcohol. A doctor has come. He does not look alarmed like the others. He looks at my tongue and holds it down with a flat stick. He listens to me with a stethoscope and holds my wrist in his fingers. I vomit while he is there. I have to take red medicine from a large spoon. It is cool in my mouth.

I dreamed that I was a hare bounding through the forest all of a night. It was a joy to run. A joy to have four swift strong legs.

One morning I woke to find a stranger looking at me with a grin. He said right off that I would have to get well or he would have nothing to do. His hair was both dark and light like a copper kettle that has been polished so that where the light catches it on a turn it is as bright as new money but leaf-brown in the shadows. His eyes were blue. Florent he said I was to call him.

He was the person Papa said was coming up for the summer. He helped me dress one morning and we went out to see his room over the stables. The sunlight looked strange. I was uncertain of my step. He had swept and scrubbed the room as clean as a box from the store. Bucket after bucket of water he'd brought up from the river and sloshed it down. All while I was being burnt out by fever and crazy with dreams that I didn't want to remember.

A camping cot with two blankets folded square and a chair and table with books were all the furniture he had. Over a dowel between two beams in a corner hung some clothes as neatly folded as maps. A rucksack. A towel and washcloth. A razor and brush. And a little silver mirror on a nail in which I saw that I had dark rings around my eyes and that my lips were as pale as a water slug.

He said he had fallen in love with our place and the woods and the river. He spoke as I'd never heard anyone speak before. He said that I needed fattening up. Something Matilda would say. He had had marvellous talks with Grandmama and was reading Swedenborg. He had combed and exercised the horses. What light. What air.

He picked me up by the armpits and put me over his shoulder like a sack. He took me down into the stable and set me on old Meg the carriage mare. He had harnessed her without a bit or reins. There was no saddle. No one had ever ridden Meg.

But there she was. Florent led her out by the bridle. I explained from my unsteady perch on her flat old back that you don't ride Meg. I saw Matilda and Thesmond watching from the door. Florent waved to them. Meg walked easily. She nudged Florent's hair. He kissed her on the nose and called her a good old girl. I laughed.

I saw Matilda poke Thesmond in the ribs. I waved to them. We went down the meadow path. It was a new world which I kept wondering if I had ever seen. After awhile Florent took his hand from the bridle so that Meg followed on her own. We wandered over the pasture. The daisies were deep and thick islands in billows of clover. Meg stopped to munch. I watched Florent's wide shoulders. He had rolled his shirt sleeves above the elbow. Papa would never do that. Or Stilt. His trousers were grey and tight like a soldier's. They tucked in an orderly way into plain scuffed rawhide hunter's boots.

We did not go near the river or the knolls.

There was milk and raisin bran cakes for us in the kitchen.

Matilda and Florent seemed to be old friends. Even Thesmond had a pleasant and familiar voice for him. Afterwards we went up and sat with Grandmama. She was having herb tea and reading Scripture. She leaned forward for me to hug her and gave me a sip of the tea and asked Florent whatever shittim wood might be. He replied that doubtless it was the acacia. The wood of which is hard and durable. She cackled with glee.

Ah! Jens.

She bobbed her head at me. All the ribbons shook on her cap. Would Stilt have given us so direct an answer? She instructed me to notice that Florent had *bon ton*.

I was ordered to bed for a nap. Florent saw me into my gown and into bed. He gave me a tap on the butt before he left. I slept easy and cool. I was not afraid to go to sleep.

Next morning we both rode Meg bareback to the sea. Florent guided her with his knees and *gee* and *haw*. He clucked at her and talked to her. Meg seemed happily bewildered by it all. She strayed to munch red berries with our indulgence and gave important switches with her tail.

We undressed on the rocks back of the beach. I liked it that he took it for granted that we would be naked as the soldiers were when they bivouacked here. I feigned indifference to his body for though he was not yet a man and therefore no longer interested in peters he was also no longer a boy. He was a naked Mohawk. He was not upholstered with flesh like the statues in the Latin book with their thick waists and bullish shoulders and womanish butts. He was trim and lean and brown. You could see my ribs.

He lifted me onto Meg and walked us in the waves. He left us to swim out beyond the breakers. I remembered the soldiers. He spooked Meg when he thrashed back and comforted her by rubbing his cheek against her muzzle.

We raced on the beach and lay in the sun. He said that I must soak up sunlight. And eat. He held my ankles for sit ups. I did them in a kind of rage. I wanted a chest as leavened as

Florent's and shoulders as knobby and broad. I wanted my
arms and legs to be as sinewy and clean of line. And as horsy
a peter and balls as plump.

We went on grand rambles. My canvas satchel and journal were in my room one morning. I wondered how they had
been retrieved and who put them there. I knew that I could not
look at the journal. I put it in a drawer and set the satchel in
the back of the closet. I did not ask how they came to be there.
No one mentioned them.

I showed Florent the drawings on the rocks. We traced
their outlines with chalk. A Viking ship with shields over the
gunwales and oars and a mast. A reindeer. A man with his
peter up. *Oho!* Florent laughed. Signs for the moon and the
sun. Shapes that might be houses. Florent said that the drawings were thousands of years old. They were drawings by the
Vikings when they sailed in dragon ships. That was the age of
bronze. We made copies and inked them in back in my room
and wrote a description of their whereabouts and sent them to
Papa.

Florent began to teach me geology. I heard about Agassiz
and Lyell and Hugh Miller.

I liked going to Florent's room above the stables. Its neat-
ness and bareness fascinated me. I was fleshing out again and
was getting to be as brown as he.

One morning when I went down to the stables Florent
had hitched Meg to the buckboard. We were going down to
the port. Matilda had packed us a lunch in a basket. I would
see what I would see when we got there. Was Papa coming
home for a visit? It was not that. Florent was not going away?
My heart went sick. Not that either. When we were out on the
turnpike going a good clip he said that my curiosity was such
a misery that it was mean not to put an end to it in spite of the
surprise. He took a paper from his pocket and handed it to me.
It was a bill of lading. I figured out its matter. One lightweight
camping tent with stays and pegs. One haversack. Two sets of

tinware mess kits. The list went on. I stared at him with a howl of delight. I hugged him. Meg tossed her head at the fuss I made.

We ate our lunch by a stream in a pleasant copse before we got to the town. Florent had a burlap half bag of oats which he held for Meg. We ate impatiently. Matilda had packed enough for four. There were sugar cubes for Meg which I fed her.

Our stuff was packaged in a large cardboard box and two smaller ones. Whole blocks of postage stamps were pasted on them. I had to sign with an indelible pencil the purple of which was proudly on my fingers for days.

We opened the boxes in Florent's room over the stables. The tent was russet and its manufacturer's name was printed on it in an elegant oval of blue lettering. Nothing was ever so wonderful. We inspected the tinware. The ropes. The pegs. My rucksack.

There was a pair of boots for me like Florent's. A twill shirt with four pockets on the front and a pocket on each of the sleeves high on the arm. And short pants just big enough to have four pockets with flaps that snapped to. Two in front. Two in back. There were but three buttons to the fly. And in foreign looking tissue wrappers with German labels were pairs of thin cotton underpants with no legs to them. Small ones for me and slightly bigger ones for Florent.

I stripped and put them on and the twill pants and pockety shirt and heavy ribbed long socks and the rawhide boots which Florent helped me with. I tried to act natural but my peter was as stiff as a bone and I blushed beet red. Florent yelled with laughter. I said in confusion that it would go down. He remarked in an easy way that I would paste myself to the sheets tonight. But a wet dream is more fun if you're wide awake helping it along with your fingers. I must have looked as if I didn't believe he was saying what he was saying. Jens! he said with a smile and the friendliest eyes in the world. Matilda and Thesmond were civilized people with an old-world sense of other people's privacy. This was his room and in it I could do whatever I wanted to whenever I wanted to. He knelt and we rubbed noses. If I ever thought he would peach on a friend I was wrong. With him I was to be free. Agreed?

Agreed. I was looking at my boots when I said it. But I looked up and sealed my words with a smile.

We went to the big house to show off my outfit. We packed the rucksack with oddments to square it into shape. I was as proud as a peacock and blushed again for being so happy. Matilda said that except for the scandalously short pants I looked like a soldier. Thesmond who studied the magazines said that I was most stylish.

I was to break the boots in by wearing them for a while every day. I tramped about in them like a wound up toy. I wore them and only the little German underpants to the beach. I chinned myself on limbs to build up my chest. Florent taught me how to walk on my hands. Most importantly he taught me how to swim in the ocean. I learned to float in the river. Breast stroke and frog kick. Not till I had got good at the crawl and scissors kick did we try the inlet. I had not known that it would be so cold.

I began to spend the night with Florent. I slept in the camper's bedroll on the floor. The night before our expedition I was so happy I walked around with nothing on but an open shirt. We had spent the afternoon checking our gear. For breakfast every morning we were to have porridge and blueberries if we were near them. Tinned evaporated milk and cocoa. Cheese and biscuits for lunch. For our dinners we would catch trout to be eaten with bran cakes made in the skillet. We also had lemons and cookies and dried fruit.

Once I stopped what I was doing to look at my peter good. I hoped in a sneaky way Florent was watching. He was not so busy that he didn't give me a hard hug one time or another.

We cleared the big house with our farewells and promises so that we could set out before dawn going north up the peninsula. Florent pointed out that we could strap up and horseshoe the bedroll over a rucksack now if we were both to sleep on the cot. There was room. We would in any case be sleeping together in the bedroll for two weeks thereafter. For the first time in my life I would not be sleeping in my gown. In a bedroll you sleep naked. Florent knew how things are done.

We undressed and laid our clothes out for the morning. Excitement scatters attention. I was wondering about wet dreams helped along by wide-awake fingers. And about sleeping beside Florent. But the camping trip crowded my mind most of all. My imagination jumped like a grasshopper. I was a mess.

Florence looked all around and said we were ready for bed.

I said I was confused.

What a goose! he said. What a wonderful goose. He held my shoulders and kneaded them and knuckled my nose and mussed my hair. His body against mine was an unfamiliar strangeness and wonderfully welcome. We were so close his peter touched my legs. I dared all and scrunched closer. He nudged my ear in response.

We untangled and lay on our backs each on the other's arm. The wadded hair under his arms smelled of dry grass and vinegar. I asked the directest question. He answered that friends can do anything they want to. He asked about my friend who had been sent to an institution. I wanted to cry. He said that I mustn't talk about my friend until I needed to. He would listen when I was ready. I was silent. He tugged my ear to show that he understood. We got snug under the blanket and fell asleep.

It was dark when Florent woke me. I could see him already dressed in the half light. I put on my clothes as he handed them to me. He tightened the buckles on my pack and I his. We oated Meg and scritched her nose and set out across the yard. We crossed the meadow in the clean cool and the knolls and bore north with the sea beginning to shine on our left. We walked at a good clip for two hours. Florent said it was wrong to have breakfast close to home and feel that we had yet to start our journey. We were in woods I'd never seen when we fancied a fine open place for our first stop. Florent made a fire in a ring of stones. We munched dried prunes while the water beaded over the fire for the porridge. I felt free and wild and important. I asked Florent if all this were real. The utter freedom. Us.

I had a vague memory of a dream in which Tarpy was naked and just out of sight of a roomful of people. Our neighbors in crinoline and Prince Alberts chatting and taking tea in the library and through the door Tarpy in the middy and ribboned hat of my sailor suit but nothing else and with the big pink acorn of his peter standing straight out. Then there was a stagecoach full of fine folk and Tarpy snake naked at the edge of the road sticking out his tongue. I liked the dream but recalled it with a chill.

Florent said he thought I'd had a wet dream and that if I were older he would know better. He stirred the porridge and we ate from the pot. We sipped our coffee sitting knee to knee looking sly quiver nimbles into each other's eyes. He tweaked my nose.

The land became rocky. The trees were taller. The light was lonelier and more northern. We caught our salmon in a swift white stream. Its meat was lovely on the tongue. The bran cakes were of my mixing and cooking by Florent's instructions. Our tent looked splendidly shipshape and cozy as it stood on its ground of larchfall. The light went gold as we were washing up and blue in the long twilight. Florent sitting against a pine filled and lit a pipe that smelled of spices and molasses. I propped myself between his knees and watched.

We talked about everything that came into our heads. I heard about the university and lectures. I learned the nature of girls. He explained socialism and free love among his student friends. I kept saying O and *why*. I undid a button of his fly and he undid a button of mine while we talked. He was surprised that I had not read the *Iliad*. It was the book he had brought. He would show me how to read it if I wanted to. He undid the next button. I countered.

A mist stretched spooky and white from bush to bush and smoked along the ground. We put more sticks on the fire and by its light we squared our quarters away and undressed. I snuggled in while Florent banked the fire with dirt. He sat crosslegged beside me on the bedroll. We heard owls as we went to sleep and unknown animals treading without caution on their rounds. The white river crashed cold over its rocks.

We were stiff from the ungivingness of our bed and stretched gratefully and naked in the pale morning warmth. We splashed clean in the dashing river and dried on the rocks with tin mugs of coffee to sip. I wanted to stay naked but Florent said that could wait until we were days further up the peninsula.

We climbed a great deal of the morning but crossed level highlands deep in strange and enormous ferns all afternoon. We saw hares and deer and the dead kingdoms of the beavers.

There was no river at our second station. We had dried beef in gravy made from an essence that came in cubes. We'd gathered wild plums yellow and tasty which we ate for dessert.

We'd cleaned and stashed our supper ware when Florent made himself comfortable with a rucksack under his shoulders. He had his pipe handy but did not light it. There was mischief in his eyes. His hand with fingers shoved between the buttons of his fly interested me greatly. Because of the sweetness of his smile I came to sit on his thighs and play the monkey with his fingers and buttons. His eyes said yes. He wrecked my hair and remarked on how the evening came on as much from below in green and blue darkenings among the trees as in a softening of departing light above. He put his hands on my legs and slid them up to my tummy and around my waist. I had unbuttoned him and made a clumsy disarrangement of everything. He pulled me to his shoulder with his cheek against my hipbone and with a heave and wiggle and two kicks got his trousers and underpants off and lowered me back to where I was. I had listened carefully over the past days to his saying that the Greek god Eros was a boy my age.

He taught me names. The head of the peter is the Latin for acorn. Its rim is the Latin for crown. Its bag with the twin eggs is the scrotum. That the sleeve is the prepuce or as the Latin translates the foreskin I knew from Scripture.

He explained while my heart was thumping at a gallop how the foreskin is like an eyelid. It too was a sensitive soft moving protector of a surface wonderfully tender. The two are where the flesh engages the spirit in its most sensual experiences.

There are our sensors of heat and cold and of textures in the world. Of sound and smell and taste. But the eye is the world. The eye and the glans or acorn are curiously alike and different. The eye is open to light. The glans is hidden except of course among lovers and frank honest people of good will. And friends.

They are like Swedenborg's heaven and hell. The healthy eye is cool and bright. The glans as you can feel is warm as blood and as dark as the inside of the body.

My mouth was as dry as the day Tarpy and I played with ourselves. Florent said in his friendliest way that if the god Eros was with us here in the dark deep of a Swedish forest and the nays of the world many miles away we would know it both by his famous cunning and his shameless boldness. Did he play with himself like a boy?

Lots. It is nature and good for the spirit. But only if Eros is running the show. Were we friends? I am if you are.

We put our foreheads and noses together and laughed. He took off my breeches. Tarpy's big business was a parsnip compared to Florent's.

I had squeezed and pulled and caressed and he had replied in kind. Eros was happily busy and inventive.

But as things got more wonderful Florent disentangled us and whistled cheerfully while he poked up the fire and put our coffee pot on to heat. I was dancing with impatience. This got me laughed at and a hug. He said we would learn to play with each other well. We would both teach the other. So we had our coffee as the dark came on. I would have liked it better if I hadn't been half out of my mind. Maybe wholly out of my mind. The second time was longer and sweeter. Florent said we were still initiates in the rites of Eros who needed to know if we were of his ilk before his magic eyes and fingers did what they do best.

The wilderness was grander day by day. The forest darker. The rocks greyer and sharper. The streams whiter and swifter. Florent taught me the Greek alphabet on our marches and I would recite it first thing every morning. He began to tell me the *Iliad*. It had all happened three thousand years ago. He told me about Schliemann and Hissarlik.

On a wide shale beach under a cliff shelved with ferns and topped with larches that went up to the sky we pitched our tent and jacked each other off for the first time in broad daylight. In spite of breaking them in my boots had made a blister on my left big toe and heel. Florent said we would give them a chance to get well. I held my foot in the cold dashing water of the stream. Florent fished above the shoals. We did our wash and laid our shirts and breeches on the clean shale to dry. Our underpants and stockings hung on the tent ropes.

Florent put a blanket in the sun and painted my blisters with iodine. I yowled. He slid his hands along my legs and rolled my balls against my crotch. He lay on his elbows and lazily worked a good feeling into my peter with his fingers. For mischief he tickled around the eyelet with his tongue. I straddled his tummy when it was time and jacked him from the front while he kept an idling hand on my peter. The second time we lay head to hip and did it together and decided that getting and giving at the same time was sort of crowded and too much of a good thing. His spunk on the tip of my finger tasted like soda and green grass. He licked some puddled in my belly button and agreed.

We explored the woods naked. We found long humps of moss that was like a deep carpet to walk over. Pitcher plants. A lady slipper all by itself. A mouse's round nest in saw grass. Snow hawks wheeling overhead. Kneedeep in a clearing of daisies and quitch grass we stood nose to nose and peter to peter. On my toes. It was a pledge.

We played leapfrog and Florent told more of the *Iliad*. We cooked our fish and oat cakes and stewed dried apples. Ruckled sooty clouds filled the sky by sunset. We got our clothes in and trenched around the tent and floored it with our rosined tarpaulin. The rain came with a whomp. I was never snugger. We sat and watched the windy warp of the downpour from the front of the tent. Our arms around each other's shoulders. While Florent sat with his knees up and smoked his pipe I lay in front of him and fiddled with his peter. I fingered and studied the conic obliquity of its nozzle. Its sumptuous vascularity. The gutty crimple of the balls. It crested as I meddled and spanged proud in my hand. I worked it into tone. You can tell by Florent's eyes and the polish of the stud. And by his saying so. I tried a boldness. I flicked my tongue against the little link of flesh that checks the underslide of the foreskin. The frenum. He liked it. He wiggled his toes and flossed my hair. He called me goose and rascal. I tongued the full contour of the glans and swivelled my lips on the flare. He throbbed and gushed. He flinched and shoved my head back. I panicked. I think he panicked. He swore. A flaw of wind worried the tent flaps. The rain slapped down in torrents.

I asked what the matter was. He didn't answer. There was just enough light to see him huddled. Biting his lip. He said *Jens*. Not *goose*. Or *chief*. But *Jens*. We sat in the dark for the longest.

Finally he scrounged in the rucksack and got something out. And something else. A candle. The tinder box. He lit the candle and set it in a tin cup between us. The rain was chilly and we put on our shirts.

He smiled at me. I think some tears had run down my cheek more from confusion than anything to cry about. Their salt mixed with the alkaline taste in my mouth. He stuffed his pipe with the cidery tobacco and lit it with the candle. I asked for a puff. I filled my mouth with the sweet smoke. My stomach listed crazily as I blew it out but I gave no sign. It was Florent too.

How the rain came down! He said he thought we had

gone too far. Was it wrong? It was wrong in that a game which we played casually for the lust of the flesh might become a bond which we could only break along with our hearts. You have already had your heart broken.

With Tarpy.

He would have to go away in less than a month. I said I thought I understood. I wasn't sure. He mentioned the world. Its disapproval. And added that for the moment the world around us was but rain. Lovely rain. Cozy rain.

I had another mouthful of pipe smoke and felt as weightless as a flaught of goose down. Florent made himself comfortable with his head on the shins of my crossed legs. I told him about Tarpy. Why I made friends with him. How I cleaned him up and gave him clothes. Florent said he knew. Papa told him.

Did he know who sent Tarpy away? He didn't know. He was sure it wasn't Papa. Who Florent said knew about our jacking off and thought it only natural. Florent said he was even mildly amused. But he had been told that Tarpy thieved and was not all there in the head. Even that Papa said was nothing Jens would take up. Jens on the contrary was no doubt a good influence on Tarpy. Florent was to see that things went well for the summer. But there was no Tarpy when he arrived. Only a very unhappy Jens.

I asked if we didn't go too far could we still jack off? Tomorrow. I added that for the distance of it. He reached up and pulled my head down to his. Nose to nose. We could go too far. Way too far. And break our hearts and be miserable but that was not now.

I squealed and wiggled onto him in a round of hugs. His legs with my arms. His chest with my legs. We rolled over. A scramble for the candle which went flying. We doused it and took off our shirts and rolled into a hug. He held my balls tight in one hand and stood my peter up with the other. His fingers were spry. Lips ticklish and delicious. Tongue slippery. His peter was as hard as duramen when I had the presence to work it with both hands. I imitated what he did. Short of choking. Our pleasure tossed and bucked to a pitch. Our pleasure. Not being given and giving but giving together and being given together. We did our best to make it last even when we knew we could catch our breath and begin again. My spunk streamed out as from a pull on an udder. Melted out first and then ran stout. The joy of it helped me bolt a deeper reach. I mashed his balls against his crotch and bore down on the swallow. He spilled out a cannikin thick and forspent. Rich. Clover and soda.

The time was important and nameless. We lit the candle and the pipe. We put on sweaters. Our hair was as messy as goblins' and we reeked of spunk. I took a fine drag on the pipe and turned pale. Florent laughed. I laughed when I could. I wobbled. We ate dried pears and apples. We peed into the rain.

We talked crazy and silly. Florent licked my peter like a puppy. Kissed me on the belly button. Wrestled me into a hug and licked me behind the ears. I wiggled free and sat on his chest and pinned his arms with my legs. His eyes shone in the candlelight. I slid backward between his thighs so that I could fool with his peter. His splendid peter. It was limber but fat. There was more neck to it than mine between the eave of the head and the ruckle of the foreskin drawn back. More bore to the keel duct. A niftier rake to the tilt of the glans. Down and up once. Twice. Thrice. And it was as tough as a plow handle. I plied the slippage with a mind to the outlandish. To be head-long generous. To outdo. I rode the foreskin full stretch with a swirl of tongue deep on the downstroke. Shallow with a flicker on the up. I put a thraw into the treadle. For style. A thropple dive plumb to the bush. A slow rippling passage. A fast bouncing passage. A jog. A trot. A sprint. When he squirmed to join up I signalled no. Lie back and feel. I was frisky and longwinded.

The rain died to a drizzle and we heard the night hunters stirring about. Our candle was almost out. A wonderful quiet replaced the drums of the rain.

I lay flatling on my elbows to charm the thronging spout to the jolt. I took my time. We had achieved *bon ton*. That was what it was. I explained to Florent that to Grandmama everything that was as it ought to be was *bon ton* or it was Swedenborgian or it was both. The very heavens were not only gardens and cities of light but the perfect and harmonious keeping of *bon ton*. Florent said that I could have fooled him. He thought we were two randy boys who had found it convenient to invent the pagan world again for their particular use and delight.

We started another candle. My peter was already in the rounce of a chime when he began its jig. He changed good for better and better for best. He stopped and started. Making it last. Making it ring to the most vibrant thrum of its resonance.

I was wonderfully sleepy afterwards and stretched and yawned with all my might. Florent opened the tent flaps. It was earliest dawn.

We walked about in the fresh half light. We got a fire going with considerable trouble but once it got cracking we heaped it high and warmed ourselves. We made porridge and coffee. The sun came out bright and strong. We made caca in the woods and bathed in the stream. The cold water shrivelled our peters and tightened our balls. I was lightheaded enough from lack of sleep and got dizzy as a drunkard on the pipe. We opened both ends of the tent to the sunshine and air. We felt clean and happy. Florent's laughing eyes and rising peter asked me if I was good for another go. We took each other's peters in our warm mouths without any jacking at all and came after a lovely long time and slept just as we were until the sun was directly above us.

Florent looked at my blisters when we woke. They were well enough for us to push on. We ate and broke camp. We packed our shirts and pants and shorts and set out in boots and rucksacks as naked as savages. I liked the flop of my peter as we walked and the sweet air and the sight of Florent. I imitated the balance of his walk. The set of his hips when he stopped. The clarity of his speech.

We walked through white birchwoods and high fields of
gorse and rocks like grazing sheep. We whistled and sang. It
was fun to pee without unbuttoning. We had not combed our
hair for days. Florent had not shaved.

We found a fine spit of land into a lake. Birches. Small
round flowers everywhere the color of egg yolk. Mossy rocks.
We pitched the tent at the tip. It was too late to fish so we had
chipped beef and bran cakes. Dried fruit. Florent was proud of
his fire and said it was a domestic animal. Man's first tamed
thing. We made a good batch of coffee. I was getting the hang
of the pipe. We passed it back and forth. We did some Greek.
Heard some of the *Iliad*.

We turned in early. We talked a long time snug and close
in the bedroll. Florent said that I fell asleep in the middle of
saying a sentence.

I would have liked a shirt at least the next morning but
bore my goose pimples without complaint. We saw deer grazing
at the edge of the wood. Two badgers loping through the bush
back to their sett for the day. We ate our midday meal on the
flat of a boulder that caught the sun in the dark of a cedar
forest. We nuzzled each other some for the fun of it after we
had lit the pipe. To show that we could be free. Florent made
me a garland of flowers and put it on my head to wear. He said
it was Greek. Something Achilles would do for Patroclus.

Each day was different. A world a day. Pine woods all of
one day. Meadows and rocks the next. The weather kept beautiful and we turned so brown that the gold hair on our arms
and legs stood out white against the dark of our skin. We were
vain of our sunbrowned peters.

It was on a promontory jutting out over a sea of treetops
that we did the most for the longest. We liked the place for its
grand view and height and floor of larch needles. There was a
rock with a dip in it just right for sheltering a fire. We found
the place in the early afternoon and decided to be lazy and stay.
There was just room for the tent among the trees. When we
were all squared away Florent said that he had never been

hornier. Which made my mouth go dry and a tickle stagger up
my peter.

Florent held up a hand. For silence. I too heard footsteps
and voices. Out here? Florent fished our underpants out of the
rucksacks. Decent enough for hunters or Lapps. We peered
over the ledge of the rock. The jingle of harness. Through the
trees we could make out a horse and wagon and someone walking alongside. So there was a trail below. We saw movement
and not shapes. A flick of yellow in the green. The nodding
head of a horse. The squeak of a wooden axle.

Florent shinnied up a tree. I admired the trim white pod
of his underpants as he climbed. The camber of his legs like a
sailor in the rigging. The bunt of his chest. The creak of the
wagon lost itself in the muddled soft sounds of the woods.

Florent said it was a medicine man and his wagon or a
travelling magician perhaps. He saw a colored sign which he
couldn't read on the side. The man on foot wore a white top
hat. He could not see who had the reins.

He dropped down and shucked his underpants. Me too.
He said that this called for coffee and pipe. Meeting another
soul in so remote a place. Coffee and pipe. I had been ready for
randy doings. Coffee was a mood with Florent. It set him study-
ing. A good fire boiled a pan of water. We had fragrant coffee
in no time. I sipped from his cup and took drags on his pipe.
Which made me giddy. I straddled his thighs so that our peters
touched. He reached under and grabbed my balls. I held the
gowpen of his. An easy clutch and good.

He knocked the pipe out and we began. It was lovely and
crazy. Twice we did each other and twice we came all tangled
together. We had supper and watched the stars come out and
the red moon. We made the tent trig with a candle. I jacked
Florent for a loving hour. For the richness of it and the long
fun. And he me except that I kept starting to shoot off and
would come a squirt which he would lick from my tummy or
his fingers and begin carefully again. Then we sank down on

each other to the hilt and grunted for sheer piggishness and drove our pleasure to the quick and swagger alone saw us through until we could loll awhile and sit on the rock passing the pipe back and forth.

What noises you hear in the deep of a forest at night. Rushes through leaves. Hoots. Caterwauls. Squeaks. Growls. Twitters. Somewhere a distant river.

Florent asked if I could possibly still be horny. I was always and forever horny. What would I like best? To be jacked off for as long as I could go. Over and over and over. He mumbled into the pipe stem. That would be better starting from scratch. I said I supposed so. Second choice. To do the same for him. Ho! he said. We had come six times each. What about a consoling scramble and a good long sleep and see tomorrow what could be done for Jens' heart's desire? He signed the promise with a kiss on my peter.

Our promontory was even finer by morning light. The forest glittered that lay below our rook. The air was lively. We rambled down after breakfast to find the road on which we had seen the horse and wagon. Two ruts in the grass was all we found of an old road overgrown. We saw where a fallen limb had been moved.

Had I perhaps heard music in the night? Music? I asked. He said that he could swear that he had heard a violin. The tune was Magyar. Then he said that next we would grow nice little kids' horns and tails and hear a frenzy of music all the time. Tabors and panpipes and clashing cymbals.

Florent stretched wonderfully and winked. He poured more coffee and lit his pipe. He patted the ground in front of him. Where I was to lie. I got comfortable with my hands under my head. Ready? he asked. Ready. His watch hung down the front of the tent on its chain. I was to signal when I was near to shooting off and we would let the urge subside. And go on. Deliciouser and deliciouser.

Florent said in his grown-up way that he imagined all this

would last maybe until lunchtime and that somebody named Jens will have had quite enough of it. There was always a tease in his grown-up voice. I said that he was never to quit. It became splendid. Sweet beyond sweet. Half an hour and my peter was as dense with sweet as the heart of a honeycomb.

We stopped for a quick stretch and pee and refiring of the pipe. I took a dizzy puff. We peed off the rock. Florent's peter was half hard and I gave it a nuzzle and kiss before we went on. Short of an hour I didn't signal fast enough and came two generous spurts which dabbed my chin and eyelid. Florent let my peter limber a bit. The tone was even finer when he recommenced. I kept the tip of my tongue between my teeth and kneaded the grass with my fingers.

He cockered along my craving with a knowing hand. He idled to a tease or took his hand away at a yummy moment or sped to the beat of a rabbit thump. In a frantic tantivy as pitched as a bolting horse I spouted a zinger that spattered us both. There were splats in the ginger down of Florent's unshaven face and a smattering down me from chin to hips. We hugged and rolled and shouted. Florent stretched and walked on his hands. We munched dried apples and stood on the rock looking out over the trees.

Then on for another wonderfully long time. After which we ate dried beef and mush and lay in the sun passing the pipe back and forth. Ready for another? Florent asked. Ready I was.

This time I too heard the violin. We cocked our ears and looked at each other. Florent said it was the same tune he had heard in the night. The carnival lilt of it came from somewhere in the forest below. Sounds carry on the wind in so quiet a place.

He went on. We achieved deliriums and idiocies of pleasure. By the middle of the afternoon I was doing Florent for we really could as I had not thought spring the bounce out of my horny pizzle. The sixth toss spavined the steed. Florent was so juicy that my hands kept slipping their grip. I tugged and bore down and just as I was beginning after a fine stretch of time to lick on some puppy laps for extra the big fellow buck-jumped a drencher full spatter all over my face. Florent sat up whooping and we rolled in a hug and squeezed and butted and crowed because we were crazy with happiness and silly beyond hope of ever being serious again.

We stretched out on the fragrant larchfall in kind warm light. I smoothed my sticky face along his tummy up to his fuzzy cheeks and lay on top of him nose to nose and eye to eye. And looked into his look.

We heard the chink of harness and the squeak of a wheel. Florent sat up and I back. We held each other's shoulders. There were voices below and a wagon. We crawled to the edge of the rock and peered down.

We saw bright colors down through the trees. I made out a flounce of orange and red that seemed to be a skirt. The wagon was a caravan all pink and yellow.

Fants! Florent said. They are fants. I said in a whisper that they looked like gypsies to me. Fants or gypsies he whispered back. Romany people. Look at the second wagon. That's the man in the white hat we saw yesterday. We could see several women in strange shawls and ruffled dresses on foot. The horses were in silver-studded harnesses. The men wore leather vests and had long moustaches. The violin! Florent whispered. There is the violin.

There were more wagons. All just below our rock. We scampered backward and got into our shorts and shirts. We pondered whether we ought to lie low. Florent pocketed his watch. We crept back to the edge.

Five wagons. Several women walking. I felt as if I were back in my place above the beach watching the gypsies looking for things the artillerymen had left behind. They were a handsome and dark people with an easy dignity to their bearing.

Florent pointed out the man with the gun and the woman with a baby at her breast. And a man in a vest all buttons.

But I saw the bear first. Behind the fourth wagon was a bear! A fat old pigeon-toed muzzled bear stepping along in a rolling lope. The man who had him on a leash carried a whip and a tambourine. I looked at Florent and Florent looked at me. A bear.

And when I looked back I saw Tarpy.

He was on the seat of the last wagon. His golden hair stood out among the gypsies like a single dandelion on a sward. I could not speak. My mouth made the shapes but not the sounds of words. I grabbed Florent's wrist. Then I remembered that he had never seen Tarpy.

*Tarpy!* I sang out.

A gypsy looked up. Florent pushed me back down from the edge of the rock.

He looked at me wildly. I had never seen his eyes so serious. I said that Tarpy was down there with them. That boy with the light hair on the last wagon is Tarpy.

Don't call again! Florent hissed at me. He had me hard by both wrists. He asked me if I was absolutely certain. I had begun to cry. I tore loose and went back to look again. A gypsy was looking up at me. But I saw only the back of the last wagon. They were all but gone by.

*Tarpy!* I hollered. *Tarpy!*

Florent pulled me back and pushed me down. I hit him as hard as I could with the sharp of my elbow against the mouth. He pinned me and held me tight.

*Let me go!* I shouted. My voice was like a rifle shot in the quiet.

We could hear the caravan rumbling on and away. *Uste!* a voice sang out. Florent turned me around and looked at me. Blood dripped from his chin. There were tears in his eyes. My mouth was open and dry. I tried to swallow but my tongue and throat were as dry as paper. I was breathing in gasps. My sides were stitched with pain.

I broke and ran. Florent tripped me and sat on me. He

held my mouth. I bit his hand. He did not move it. I kicked. *Jens!* he said quietly. We will follow them and see if it really is Tarpy. But we can't put ourselves at the mercy of such people. They are thieves. They would think nothing of taking everything we have. They would think nothing of killing us out here miles from anywhere.

I hated him. I wouldn't look at him when he turned me loose. I walked away into the trees. I was barefoot and my heart hurt. My stomach was a tight knot pinching in. I cut and ran. O did I run! I sprang over big rocks without looking. I plunged through bushes. I suddenly had all the strength in the world and no end to it ever in sight. I had something keen and fine that I had never had before. There was nothing that could stop me. I could fly if need be. Nothing could puzzle me. Nothing dared puzzle me. I knew how to circle and come out exactly where the gypsies were. I was God knows where in a thick and tall wood but I was not lost. I ran like a rabbit. Whether Florent was following me I couldn't be bothered to stop and find out and moreover didn't care. I would never see him again.

I ran and ran and ran. The world was nothing to me. The world was merely something negligible underfoot. Something to brush aside. I even knew when I had to begin to be cautious. I had to see the gypsies before they saw me. Florent had put the doubt in my mind that I might have seen not Tarpy but someone I mistook for Tarpy at that distance through branches. Yet I knew that it was Tarpy. Only when I slowed down to a jog crossing a stream with a tearing splash and running up a long boulder like a monkey and jumping from the other side without the least fear of what I would come down on did I begin to think how Tarpy could be with the gypsies. He had escaped from the institution or had been let out. He had joined the gypsies. The gypsies had stolen him.

I knew I was near and began to look to the noise I was making. But the wood came upon no opening. No road.

I stopped. I listened.

I knew my mind. Knew that my body was in absolute control. I could run a hundred miles. I could climb the highest tree and jump down. I could hear for miles. I could call to Tarpy from where I was if I was so minded. My cocked ears heard the jingle and clop of horses I knew I would hear.

I crept forward. I made haste slowly. I commanded the bushes not to betray me with sounds. Finally I got a glimpse of a wagon. The gypsies seemed to be pulling into a clearing. I heard their voices. I was close enough to see a horse being unharnessed from its traces.

Then without any warning my knees began a spasm of trembling and I was cold all over with sweat. I had sense enough to know that it was because I had no notion what in the world to do next. I hated Florent even more deeply for planting the doubt. If it was not Tarpy I could run. I knew I could run. If it was Tarpy he would know what to do.

*Who are you?* a voice said and I jumped with a sickening stab of fear.

A gypsy woman was laughing at me. She had slipped up behind me. She was carrying firewood. Her smile showed long white crooked teeth. Gold bangles across her forehead and throat and rings in her ears. She was old and marvellously wrinkled.

Boy! she said. Who are you and what you want? Fright not. *Eh! Uva tu?*

I stammered Tarpy's name. *Jeg talar inte mycket svenska. Tarr pi?* When I pointed to the wagons she took me by the hand so that I arrived as a curiosity led sheepishly among the gathering gypsies by a tall woman who seemed to take enormous pleasure in surprising everybody by turning up not only with a bundle of sticks for the fire but with a barefoot boy drenched with sweat and trembling as well.

A man in a bandana squatted before me and studied me with wide eyes. I looked wildly for Tarpy.

And saw him.

He was with two gypsy boys in red shirts. He was himself in gypsy dress. An orange blouse. His eyes looking at me were eyes in a dream. He stared with a strange concern as if he had known me a hundred years ago and could recall my face but not my name.

*Tarpy!* I saw you from a rock down the road! I called but you didn't hear me.

He kept looking at me. One of the boys in a red shirt said something in gibberish. Tarpy answered him but not me.

The old woman came between us. You know him? she said to me. You know our *gadjo niglo?*

*Tarpy!* I said again. I was determined to have him answer to the name.

The old woman spoke to him. Her voice rose and made a kind of song. It was the voice grown-ups wheedle children with. But it was a kind and good-natured voice. She had a jolly way about her.

She turned to me with lifted hands. But he says he knows you never! she sang out. How can it be?

My eyes were blind with tears. I looked at the old woman and looked at Tarpy. My hands trembled. I went to Tarpy and searched his face. Could I be wrong? I blubbered. Tarpy looked at me with interest and then smiled at the boys in the red shirts. He turned his hands palms up as if to ask the gypsies if he could be held responsible for this unseemliness.

*Tarpy!* I shouted.

He turned away.

A man took me by the arm. I realized that it was night. Fires crackled and flared. A ring of gypsies parted for us to pass through. I was being led away. Many of the faces were kind.

I had no sense of wanting to say anything to anybody and no curiosity as to where I was being led or as to what I was next to do. We stopped at the steps of a caravan where an old man sat holding a carved staff.

*Gadjo!* he laughed. You have known our gold-haired

*niglo*? He is now a *rom*. Forgive him he cannot to you come back. He can say *na janav ko dad m'ro has. Miro gule dai merdyas*. The *gadji* beat him and starved him. We are better people. He has now mother and father. Like you he has a brother.

He raised his hand. And there was Florent. He wore one rucksack and carried the other. My boots were under his arm.

Florent gave me a hard look. He took two *kronor* out of his shirt pocket and offered them to the old man. Who closed his ancient hand upon them with a complacent smile. He raised his staff as if in farewell. Florent threw my boots and stockings at my feet.

I put them on in confusion. He handed me my rucksack but did not help me strap it on.

A gypsy said that we could not walk in the dark.

Florent replied that we could walk in the dark.

We had trudged along what I supposed to be the overgrown road for quite awhile before I noticed we were walking in rain. Florent was ahead. I simply followed. My rucksack rode sloppily in the small of my back and my stockings were ruckled messily in my boots. My hair streamed down into my eyes. We plodded on without any word or sign between us. The night was very dark.

I turned my ankle and fell sprawling but scrambled up as quickly as I could find my balance. Florent walked on in indifference. It was so dark that I could only hear him. Hear his measured and even tread. My rucksack was askew. I had to run to catch up. Never knowing where I was stepping. I could feel my face pinch up to cry and fight back the sting of tears and taste their salt in my mouth. I was soaked through to the skin. So must Florent be.

We had got into muddy ground where my boots sank into slush. I could hear Florent's boots sucking in and out of mire. The mud showed me how tired I was. My legs ached. My back ached. My nose ran. Water dripped off my fingers.

Florent went on. I followed.

I began to shiver. A pain across my shoulders made me gasp. My feet had turned to lead and were like cakes of ice.

The rain let up to a drizzle and stopped altogether at a moment I did not notice. A false dawn came grey in the east. I began to make out Florent's back. We seemed to be climbing a hill. I fell on my knees and skinned them and felt a lash of fire across them as I forced myself up. Florent was at the top of the hill in full outline against the cold grey of the sky.

Thank God he was standing still. He was taking off his rucksack. He spoke for the first time. He ordered me to gather sticks. Small sticks from under trees and dry ones if I could find them. He was on his knees blowing on a heap of leaves and twigs when I came back with sticks most of which were wet. He ordered me to lay out the tarpaulin and take off my clothes and get into the bedroll.

Carefully he nurtured the fire. He brought bigger sticks. Dawn and the fire showed me that he was as wet as if he had just climbed out of a river. The fire cracked and lept and danced tall. It was practically a bonfire as he piled on more and bigger sticks. Then he stripped. He dried his hair with a shirt from the rucksack and tossed the shirt to me with orders to dry my hair. We stood naked at the fire red in its light. Florent's underlip was split and swollen ugly.

He handed me slices of dried fruit. Its taste was a kind of blessing. He saw my knees and painted them with iodine. Too tired to stand any more I sat on the bedroll.

Was it Tarpy? Florent asked.

I said that he had refused to recognize me. It was Tarpy all right. Could they have done something to him that he wouldn't know me?

Florent squatted by the sinking fire. He said that they had taken him in. Had given him a home.

I was too tired to think or answer. I fell asleep before Florent joined me in the bedroll. Never had I been so grateful for warmth and rest and sleep.

We woke at noon and packed and set out as if we were in

a hurry. Florent's split lip throbbed so much that I could see it pulse. He did not mention it. We did not talk. We made camp early and slept as soon as we had eaten dried beef which we did not bother to heat.

Florent asked next day if I wanted to go home. I supposed so. We were tired of each other's company.

Far into the next day deep in a forest with patches of wild flowers and a racket of wind splashing the highest branches together and the smell of green and earth as fresh in the nose as baking bread or butter risen in the churn I asked him to tell me more of the *Iliad*. He did not answer me.

We had a hot supper that night. He lit his pipe for the first time after I had seen Tarpy with the gypsies but did not offer it to me. His lip was healing. We slept back to back in the bedroll.

Our hikes were like a trial of strength. Except for brief rests we walked all day and fell asleep dead tired every night. We reached woods familiar to me. One afternoon we saw the big house in its valley. We were back.

There were carriages I did not recognize in the drive. I saw Papa through a window and Matilda ran out to fold me in her arms and call me dear soul and say that Grandmama had died in her sleep. I wept horribly. Bitterly.

I wanted to see her. She had been buried a week. Papa took me to her grave at the church. There were flowers in vases tilted at crazy angles on the grave. She shared a tombstone with Grandpapa whom I never knew and the date of her death had already been chiselled in raw and white beside her birth-date as dim as the weathered stone itself.

Florent appeared in the drawing room next day dressed to travel. He would take the stage to the port. He shook hands with Papa and Matilda and Thesmond. He shook hands with me.

I went out to watch the buckboard take him away. Nock was at the reins. I wandered down by the stable and across the front meadow. I crossed the knolls. The stage took up passen-

gers where our road met the turnpike. I began to run for fear
that he had timed it all so that Nock and the buckboard would
still be there when the stage came.

But Florent was alone with his bags under the oak across
from the ostler's house when I came up behind him. He turned
when I was near and about to call his name. He walked up to
me expressionless and hugged me as tight as he ever had. *Forgive me* he said so quietly at my ear that I had to think what
he had said. Forgive you?

But the stage was rolling to a halt and the guard was
sounding his horn. He gathered his bags under his arm and
crossed the road. I waved to him as the coach thundered away.

I saw him once afterwards at the university but we did
not speak.

# Author's Notes

AUGUST BLUE   is a painting by Henry Scott Tuke (1858–1929) in the Tate Gallery, London. It was painted in 1893.

*Yeshua*: Aramaic for Joshua, the Greek for which, *Iesous*, became the Latin *Jesus*. The source for this anecdote is an uncanonical Gospel of Thomas (*The Apocryphal New Testament*, translated by M. R. James, Oxford University Press, 1924, revised 1953). I have supplied a lacuna in the text with a poster from Heimish House (1978) depicting an alef. Its text ("A Yud above, the Creator; a Yud below, the Jewish People; a Vav, Torah & Mitzvos, uniting them") is adapted from the works of Rabbi Schneur Zalman of Liadi.

*Sylvester*: I am indebted to L. S. Feuer's "America's First Jewish Professor: James Joseph Sylvester at the University of Virginia," *American Jewish Archives*, vol. 36, no. 2 (1984), and to the California Institute of Technology department of Mathematics.

*As we descended westward . . . Ely Minster:* This passage is an amalgam of descriptions by Samuel Pepys and Daniel Defoe (*A Journey Thro' the Whole Island of Great Britain*, 1724–1726) of the Isle of Ely in Cambridgeshire where Ludwig Wittgenstein is buried.

*Colonel Lawrence:* His visit to Tuke at Falmouth in 1922 is unattested except by Tuke's painting of him as Aircraftsman Ross at Clouds Hill.


BELINDA'S WORLD TOUR   Ronald Hayman records in his *Kafka: A Biography* (Oxford, 1981) that "One day in the street [Kafka] saw a little girl, crying because she had lost her doll. He explained that the doll, whom he had just met, had to go away but promised to write to her. For weeks afterwards he sent her letters in which the doll described her travel adventures." My story is a conjectural restoration of these presumably lost letters.

GUNNAR AND NIKOLAI
*punktum punktum*: a rhyme by L. Albeck Larsen in *Punktum punktum komma streg*, a Carlsen Pixi Pege Bog (Copenhagen, 1981). *Conventional psychology . . . life and sensibility*: George Santayana, *The Realm of Essence*, Charles Scribner's Sons, 1937.

AND  A papyrus fragment from an early second-century gospel, published in 1935 by Sir Harold Idris Bell and T. C. Skeat, collected in Appendix I to M. R. James's *The Apocryphal New Testament*, cited above.

THE LAVENDER FIELDS OF APTA JULIA  A photograph by Bernard Faucon shows the family wash hung against a lavender field, making a pun on the Old French *lavanderie* (laundry) and *lavande* (lavender). Another of his photographs is of a playhouse in the form of a boxcar made by children of scrap lumber.

THE KITCHEN CHAIR  The sentence is in *Home at Grasmere: Extracts from the Journal of Dorothy Wordsworth (written between 1800 and 1803) and from the Poems of William Wordsworth*, edited by Colette Clark, Penguin Books, 1960.

THE CONCORD SONATA
*Thoreau did not love nature . . . this beautiful parable in Walden*: John Burroughs, *The Complete Writings*: Volume V: *Indoor Studies*, William H. Wise & Co., New York, 1924.
*I have no new proposal . . . desire itself*: Stanley Cavell, *The Senses of Walden*, North Point Press, 1981.
*And yet we did unbend . . . that afternoon*: Thoreau, *A Week on the Concord and Merrimac Rivers*, 1849.
*Mencius*: The passage in Mencius that Thoreau exfoliated into his beautiful paragraph about having lost a hound, a bay horse, and a dove is at Book VI, Chapter XI (in James Legge's *The Works of Mencius*):

> Mencius said: Benevolence is man's mind, and righteousness is man's path.

How lamentable it is to neglect the path and not pursue it, to lose this mind and not know how to seek it again!

When men's fowls and dogs are lost, they know to seek for them again, but they lose their mind, and do not know to seek for it.

The great end of learning is nothing else but to seek for the lost mind.

Thoreau read Mencius in M. G. Pauthier's translation, *Les quatre livres de philosophies morale et politique de la Chine*, Paris, 1841. For Legge's *mind* one ought nowadays to read *inborn nature*.

*I remember years ago . . . the birds*: Henry D. Thoreau, "The Dispersion of Seeds," in *Faith in a Seed: The Dispersion of Seeds and Other Late Natural History Writings*, edited by Bradley P. Dean Island Press / Shearwater Books, Washington, D.C. and Covelo, California, 1993.

MELEAGER   The geometry is from the *Encyclopaedia Britannica*, first edition, 1771.